"So It *Is* Mutual,"

Jack said huskily, a half-smile curving the corners of his mouth. "At last you've admitted you want me as much as I want you."

Cassie badly needed support. She turned and rested her elbows on the fender of the jeep, lowering her head to her hands. Lord, what had possessed her to succumb to this man in this moment? She didn't love him—she didn't even like him!

It was that tenderness he'd just shown the tiny gazelle he'd freed from the snare. She wanted the same gentling and salvation for herself. Divorcee, she spat silently at herself, divorcee hungry for love . . . from anyone!

Dear Reader:

We've had thousands of wonderful surprises at SECOND CHANCE AT LOVE since we launched the line in June 1981.

We knew we were going to have to work hard to bring you the six best romances we could each month. We knew we were working with a talented, caring group of authors. But we *didn't* know we were going to receive such a warm and generous response from readers. So the thousands of wonderful surprises are in the form of letters from readers like you who've been kind with your praise, constructive and helpful with your suggestions. We read each letter...and take it seriously.

It's been a thrill to "meet" our readers, to discover that the people who read SECOND CHANCE AT LOVE novels and write to us about them are so remarkable. Our romances can only get better and better as we learn more and more about you, the reader, and what you like to read.

So, I hope you will continue to enjoy SECOND CHANCE AT LOVE and, if you haven't written to us before, please feel free to do so. If you have written, keep in touch.

With every good wish,

Sincerely,

Carolyn Nichols

Carolyn Nichols
SECOND CHANCE AT LOVE
The Berkley/Jove Publishing Group
200 Madison Avenue
New York, New York 10016

P.S. Because your opinions *are* so important to us, I urge you to fill out and return the questionnaire in the back of this book.

Second Chance at Love

PRIMITIVE SPLENDOR
KATHERINE SWINFORD

SECOND CHANCE AT LOVE
BOOK

Second Chance at Love books are published by
The Berkley/Jove Publishing Group,
200 Madison Avenue, New York, NY 10016

Chapter One

CASSANDRA DEARBORN RACED down the Nairobi street. Her honey gold hair streamed out behind her and her cheeks were flushed a deep red. Her beautiful pale gray eyes were wide with anxiety. Though she had a tomboy's athletic body, she'd been running for a long time and was nearly out of breath. She held her expensive German camera in one hand to keep it from jostling her breasts, but her photography equipment case was hanging free. It banged cruelly into the side of her leg with every stride she took. Still she ran on as fast as she could.

Turning abruptly onto the main boulevard, she almost ran headlong into a Kikuyu woman who was carrying a load of firewood.

"I'm sorry. I didn't see you. I'm sorry," she panted. Then she ran on with a final wave at the woman, who stared curiously.

But she was almost there. Cassie glanced at her watch. She was fifty minutes late and time was money, every precious aggravating second of it.

She bolted across the road and was almost hit by a safari outfitter's zebra-striped minibus. The driver leaned angrily on the horn, but Cassie ignored him. She went up the steps to the luxury hotel two at a time and burst through the door into the lobby.

Once inside she looked around and saw exactly what she had feared. Everyone from the magazine was there waiting. Kate and Monica, the two models, had perched

1

their long frames on top of a pile of suitcases. Monica was stifling a yawn. Douglas Tyler, the editor, was cooling his temper with a martini, as was the hairdresser, Barry. The only ones who didn't seem put out were Douglas's secretary Jill and the set stylist, Max. They'd just fallen madly in love and spent this time as they spent every other waking moment, staring deep into each other's eyes.

There was another man in the group who Cassandra didn't know and assumed must be the driver who'd come to take them all to the Hillside Resort. He was standing with his back to her. Cassie could see that he was a tall man, at least six three or four. His lean, muscular frame was accentuated by the khaki slacks and matching safari shirt he wore. One hand rested on his hip in an arrogant gesture. His shirtsleeves were rolled up and when Cassie noticed the fine veins and hard muscles on his arm, she felt a little jolt in her stomach. Then she smirked at her own reaction. She'd leave this man to the models. They went for the animalistic chauffeur types. She had far more important things to do.

Barry had finished his martini and was staring unhappily into the glass. "When the hell can we get out of here?" he was asking as Cassie approached.

"As soon as that idiot Mrs. Dearborn gets here," answered the driver in a clipped British accent.

Cassie knew she was in the wrong but she'd never taken insults easily. She stepped forward defiantly. "That idiot is here."

There was a stir through the group. The driver turned around to face her. His shirt was open, revealing the hard curve of his chest and his dark, wavy hair was just slightly in need of a cut, which gave him a wild and threatening look in spite of his chiseled aristocratic features. Cassie felt her throat tighten. It wasn't just the physical presence of the man that disturbed her. It was his eyes. They were a rich but icy blue. A man with those eyes had to be cunning, resourceful, and used to getting his way. Cassie had only known one other person who had eyes like that, her former husband.

She wanted to back away and she would have if she'd been alone with the man. But she couldn't, not with Douglas Tyler standing right there. Although Cassie hadn't been in the fashion business long, she had learned one very valuable lesson—it was fatal to show any sign of weakness.

Holding firm, she locked into the driver's gaze. She sensed that some sort of apology was in order but she wasn't about to make one. She might have if he'd been a different sort of person, but he seemed very imperious and Cassie had had enough of imperious men to last a lifetime. She tried to think of something that would make him stop looking at her like that, something that would put him in his place.

"I didn't mean to keep you waiting," she said levelly. "I'll make it up to you in your tip."

The man raised an eyebrow. He seemed to be amused by what she'd said, which infuriated her.

"My dear young woman," he said, not taking his eyes off her, "my time is very valuable. I trust you'll come up with a suitable sum."

Cunning she had expected; avariciousness she hadn't. But then her husband had been greedy so she should have known this man would be too.

"Whatever," she said curtly. "Fifty dollars should be sufficient, shouldn't it?"

"Dollars?" he said. "We use Kenyan shillings here."

"Then go to the bank and change it," she snapped.

With an easy smile, the man calmly ran his eyes along her body. "I guess I'll have to. Unless, of course, you'd care to make this little transaction in some other coin?"

Cassie felt her anger rising. She didn't like the sexual

innuendo at all and decided to put an end to the conversation. Since the man was so greedy, the best way to do that seemed to be to appeal to his pocket. "The longer you keep haggling with me, the more I'm likely to lower that tip."

At this he laughed. "By all means, I certainly wouldn't want to lose such a lavish sum." Then he turned away from her and looked back at the rest of the group. "Let's go then."

As the driver motioned to the bellboys to load up the suitcases, wardrobe, and other equipment, Cassie breathed a sigh of relief. Her plan had worked: he seemed to be letting her alone. She hoped that he would only be their driver for this leg of the trip, for she didn't think she could bear him the whole time. Certainly she was under enough pressure with her job as it was. If they really intended to keep this man on for the duration, she and Douglas would have to have a little chat.

She was about to go outside and climb into the small bus that was waiting out front when she remembered to her horror that she hadn't packed. She'd been so eager to get out and take some pictures of Nairobi this morning that she'd left scattered around the room the clothes she had worn on the flight in, her nightie, and a couple of outfits that she'd put on this morning but decided not to wear. Instantly she realized how foolish she had been to try to do some of her own work this morning. Not only had the decision made her late, it had also left her totally unprepared to leave. Since this was only her second really big photography assignment, she couldn't afford to make any other mistakes. If she did she'd probably ruin her reputation and her chance for a solid career. She'd been hired to work for the magazine, and from now on she would limit her activities to the job she was paid to do. She would pack her clothes, get on the bus, and stick strictly to business. She sighed heavily, took a deep breath and walked up to the driver boldly.

"I haven't packed yet."

Again he gave her the grin that made her so uncomfortable, and then said, "I know."

Her nostrils flared, but she managed to speak politely. "You'll have to wait for me while I get my things together."

"It's been taken care of. Get in the bus."

"I don't think you understood me. My suitcases aren't down here yet."

"Yes, they are," he said, looking intently at Cassie with those cold blue eyes.

Feeling her temper rise higher, she took a deep breath. "Well, there must have been a mistake. I still have some things in my room."

"Actually, you don't. Your friend Monica Peyton and I packed your clothes and we made a thorough search to see that nothing was left behind."

The thought of this man handling her personal things made her pale with rage. "You didn't!" she cried.

"Oh, but we did," he drawled. "I can promise that I went through your room thoroughly and nothing escaped my eyes. However, if you don't believe me, I think I can give you an inventory of most if not all of the items we packed."

"I'm sorry, but I . . ."

Cassie's words were cut off as he continued; "Item: One rather diaphanous cotton negligee. Item: A rather chic pair of woman's lavender slacks and shirt to match. Item: One small gold travel alarm inscribed 'To my precious Cassandra from her loving husband.'"

Before she could stop herself Cassie blurted out, "My ex-husband. It's not Mrs. Dearborn. It's Ms."

Again, he raised that quizzical brow. "I see."

"The stupid clock still works. Why shouldn't I use it?"

"My dear," he said with sarcasm in his voice but a sudden kindness in his eyes, "I couldn't possibly respond to that question unless we were on much more intimate terms."

"That is something we will never be," she said quickly.

The coldness returned to his expression as he went on, "I almost forgot one further item—various rather skimpy bits of feminine lingerie. Singularly inappropriate for African terrain and climate. But then, I suppose that you have your purpose for bringing along that particular gear."

Cassie didn't like what he was implying, not one bit. Nor did she like the idea of this man going through her intimate apparel. "I should sue you," she said.

"You were very late and Douglas Tyler suggested someone pack your gear. What he says goes, doesn't it?"

"That doesn't give *you* the right to paw over my lingerie!"

"Believe me," he said, "I really had no intention of doing that. I'd asked Miss Peyton to take care of those things but she wasn't as much help as I'd hoped."

Cassie couldn't say anything. She was feeling too riled up now . . . and too vulnerable suddenly. They'd just flown from New York to London to Kenya yesterday, an exhausting flight, and she felt drained and over-emotional. She wished she weren't so tired that she couldn't think of a snappy one-liner to get out of this conversation. Normally, she was sure, one would have popped into her mind.

Finally the driver broke the silence. "The others are all on the bus. I don't think we should keep them waiting any longer."

Cassie nodded and followed him outside. But she couldn't resist getting in just one last dig. "I'm glad you itemized everything you packed," she said in a mock-sweet tone. "I'll know who to look for if I find that anything has been stolen."

He shot an amused glance at her over his massive shoulder. "Fortunately, I'm not in the habit of wearing women's clothing so I think you'd find it a bit difficult to prove a motive."

Cassie didn't find that remark the least bit funny.

"You really must develop a sense of humor, *Ms*. Dearborn," he said.

Cassie didn't answer, but she did note with satisfaction his emphasis on the term "Ms."

When they got to the bus, all the seats were filled except for the driver's seat and the one next to it. The driver opened the door for her and Cassie realized she had no choice but to endure his nearness for the first leg of the trip at least. She was sure when they stopped that she could persuade one of the models to trade seats with her.

The driver started the motor and they drove off through the streets of Nairobi. Cassie stared out the window so she wouldn't have to see him even from the corner of her eye. Behind her the group chattered away. Monica was asking Barry about a conditioner for her hair; Kate was telling Doug about her new boyfriend back home in the States; Max and Jill were, of course, snuggling, kissing, and whispering in the very back. In spite of all the other noise, Cassie was mainly aware of the heavy silence of the man sitting next to her.

Even as the city sped by, she remained upset about their encounter in the hotel. She knew she'd been a little highhanded, but then he had provoked her by being so arrogant. At last, though, she shrugged off the episode as an inevitable clash of personalities and gave her real attention to the city through which they passed. There was far more to Nairobi than just the marketplace she'd been photographing earlier that morning. It was obviously a city of contrasts. Luxury hotels and elegant office buildings were scattered all through the downtown area, yet certain blocks consisted of simple small rectangular homes or rows of tin and wood shacks. However, even in the poorer areas nothing appeared to be dirty or depressing. And the people seemed to be light-hearted and industrious. There was an enthusiasm about the way they did things that Cassie liked.

She rolled down her window, remarking again that the air felt cool and pleasant. At first the temperate climate had puzzled her, because she knew Kenya was right on the equator. Then she'd learned from a crew member that most of Kenya was on a high plain and it was the altitude which made the climate so pleasant.

Suddenly the bus lurched around a corner and onto a road that was still under construction. Cassie was jolted against the driver's hard muscular thigh and shoulder. He looked down at her leaning against him and a little smirk played around the corners of his lips. As he turned back to look at the road, she quickly straightened herself up again.

"Sorry about that," he called out to the others in the back.

"Well, watch it, why don't you?" Monica said irritably.

"Oh, I knew that bad turn was there," the driver said suavely. "I just forgot to warn you."

"Next time don't forget." Monica's voice quavered as they bounced over the rough roadbed. "I mean, I almost bruised my leg on the door handle that time. Do you realize how ridiculous I'd look modeling shorts with a big old black and blue mark?"

"Again, my apologies," the driver said.

Everyone was getting bumped around in the bus. Even Max and Jill had stopped kissing and were looking around uncomfortably.

Doug leaned forward and tapped the driver on the shoulder. "Jack?"

Still keeping his eyes on the road the driver angled his head so that he could hear better. Cassie made a mental note of the name "Jack." Now she would know who to refer to if it really became necessary to ask Doug to get rid of this arrogant, forward driver.

"Jack," Doug continued, "couldn't we take another road?"

"I thought you wanted to make up some time since Ms. Dearborn was so late," Jack said. Cassie felt herself redden. "This is a short cut."

"It's pretty rough on the girls," Doug said, nodding toward the two models.

"Well, they'd better get used to it for the back country," Jack insisted. "Besides, it's not too much longer on this. Then we hit the main road to Hillside."

Doug sat back in his seat. They all jostled along for a few more minutes until the driver turned them around another sharp corner. This time he did remember to warn them and Cassie held the door handle firmly so she wouldn't slide against him. Right after that, they merged onto a smooth, hard-topped highway which led them out toward the hills.

Several miles up the road they passed a small village of round thatched huts. There was a bustle of activity among the villagers. Cassie was especially struck by the beauty of the women. They were dressed in brightly colored, patterned robes, like long dashikis. Cassie had always thought the dashiki a West African style, but obviously it had caught on here as well. She wanted to ask about the origin of the dashiki, but then she realized that the only one who would be able to answer her question was Jack. She certainly didn't want to start a conversation with him.

Apparently, Monica had also been struck by the village women's costumes. She pressed her nose against the glass, "Oh my stars! Look, Kate! I can't go home without one of those gorgeous dresses!"

"How elegant!" Kate said as she looked out, too.

"That's a Kikuyu village," Jack said.

"Huh?" Monica asked.

"The Kikuyu are the largest tribe in Kenya. They're very enterprising, warm-hearted people. The more you get to know them, the better you'll like them. This is a fairly typical country village."

"In what sense?" Doug asked.

"Just the way it's laid out," Jack answered. "Central group of huts. Shambas and cattle grazing land on the outskirts."

"What's a shambas?" Kate asked.

"That's Swahili for fields," Jack told her.

"I see," Kate said. Then she went back to talking with Doug.

Jack was quiet and so was Cassie. Eventually, the road wound up and up the plain until they were traveling through rolling hills.

Finally the driver spoke. "This is Hillside."

"Where?" Kate asked.

"We're only at the outskirts. Down below is the private game reserve."

"Oh!" Monica cried. "I don't see how anyone could shoot those cute little animals."

Cassie glanced at the driver quickly, to see how he would react. She herself had always been an animal lover and was very much in favor of saving endangered species. This driver seemed like the rough type who might go in for poaching on the side to raise a little extra money. If he dared to make fun of Monica's statement, Cassie was prepared to start a hell of an argument with him.

As she watched, that odd smile crossed his face again, and Cassie braced herself for a sarcastic remark. But instead he said, "I couldn't agree with you more, Miss Peyton. Actually, the Hillside game reserve is more of what you Americans call a wildlife refuge. No shooting is allowed."

To Cassie's amazement, she noticed that her heart was pounding and her stomach churning. She was shocked to see how physically upset she'd been over the prospect of arguing with this man, and was relieved that she hadn't actually had to follow through with her promise to herself to defend wildlife preservation. Her palms were clammy. Discreetly, she tried to rub them dry against the car seat.

The driver turned to her and said in a low voice, "You seem agitated, Ms. Dearborn."

Cassie looked at him in surprise. She recovered quickly, though. "Jet lag. It gets to the best of us."

"Ah, I see," the driver said with just a touch of sarcasm. "Here I thought you were distraught over the prospect of losing fifty American dollars."

"Hardly," said Cassie. Turning away, she frowned at the amount of the tip she'd promised him. It had been an extravagant gesture, especially now that she was out on her own again. But then she was willing to pay a large price to maintain her pride.

They drove farther and farther up, until Hillside was finally ahead of them. Cassie couldn't help gasping at the beauty of the place. Everywhere she looked there were flowers. She only recognized some of them—bougainvillea, hibiscus, oleanders. There were countless other flowers that she didn't know. In the distance were rows of trees which she assumed must be part of the Hillside coffee plantation about which she'd read.

The resort itself was much smaller than she'd expected. She'd always thought that any place so famous would have to be a huge complex. However, the main structure was only a two story building. It was made of wood and glass, very elegantly and simply designed, but not terribly large. Surrounding the main building were about a dozen thatched huts like the ones they had seen in the village. Cassie knew from her travel itinerary that these huts were fitted with modern conveniences and were rooms for tourists.

The driver pulled up in front of the main building and stopped the bus.

"Here we are," he said as he got out.

Immediately, two porters came and opened the doors for the rest of the party. As everyone gathered around to get their room assignments, Cassie pulled some bills out of her purse and walked over to the driver. She tapped him on the shoulder and held out the money.

To her astonishment, he started to laugh and pushed the money away. "My dear Ms. Dearborn, that's hardly necessary."

"A promise is a promise," Cassie said, still holding out the money.

"But I think I may have goaded you into it," he said with a sarcastic smile. "I've been known to have a rather difficult sense of humor."

Cassie could feel herself getting edgy again; she just wanted to give him the money and get out of there.

"Take it," she said in a stern voice.

"I will under one condition. That you join me for a bottle of champagne in the bar. I'm sure that your fifty dollars will be enough to cover the cost."

Cassie pressed the money into his hand and felt his powerful fingers close around the bills.

"I take it this means you accept."

Cassie shook her head and stepped away. She'd given him the tip and she was through with him. She didn't intend to exchange more than the briefest civilities with him from this moment on.

The driver slowly looked her over before he spoke

again and Cassie was annoyed with herself that she actually felt uncomfortable under his gaze.

"Surely," he began with a drawl, "surely, any young woman who calls herself 'Ms.' is liberated enough to have a drink with a stranger."

Again, there was that sexual innuendo—no! that tone of seductiveness—in his voice which irritated her no end. She looked him in the eye with the coldest expression she could manage, then turned on her heel and went off to get her room assignment. As she walked away she thought she heard him chuckling softly.

In her room Cassie peeled off her jeans and T-shirt. Her body still felt sticky after that long run from the marketplace to the hotel. She went into the bathroom and turned on the shower. As she adjusted the temperature, she couldn't help noticing how charming the room was. The tub and shower were separate and done in large white tile. On some of the tiles were African motifs, painted by hand with a charming simplicity. The shower curtain was made from an elegant batik fabric.

She stepped under the spray. At first, she gave herself a moment to get used to the water. Then she put her head under the nozzle and stood there for a few minutes, feeling the warm water begin to relax her knotted muscles. Realizing how tense she was, Cassie decided to stay under the shower until she felt herself unwind, and finally she was calm enough to think things through.

There were professional...and personal reasons for her to be on edge. The most obvious one was the job ahead of her. It was considered the plum assignment of the fashion industry. She would be traveling all through Kenya and Tanzania, shooting the summer sportswear layout for a top fashion magazine. Every good photographer in New York had been vying for the job, but Cassie had gotten it. Even a seasoned pro would feel pressured to turn in excellent work, and as a newcomer Cassie was under much more pressure.

The first photography assignment for the magazine had been given to her as a favor to her ex-husband, Larry. It was an awkward situation and Cassie had felt uncomfortable, but she needed the break so she'd taken the job. Besides, she knew why Larry had gotten it for her: this was his way of thanking her for not costing him much for the divorce. His two previous wives had demanded huge alimony payments, whereas Cassie hadn't taken anything but the clothes he'd bought her. She'd even returned the jewelry, the champagne colored mink coat with matching fox collar and cuffs, and the collection of valuable originals by the early master photographers. In return for her consideration, Larry had put in the call to Douglas Tyler which set her up with one of the best fashion magazines in the world.

As she poured out some scented shampoo and worked it through her hair, Cassie thought about her divorce. Surely, she had to admit that that was partly the cause of her anxiety. After all, the decree had just been made final three days before she left for Kenya. She'd been legally separated from Larry for a year and they'd worked together to see that the divorce went through without any trouble. However, it had still come as a shock when she'd actually gotten the letter in the mail. Cassie had felt frightened, which wasn't at all the way she'd expected to feel.

To make matters worse, as soon as she'd come here she'd met that man with the same kind of cold blue eyes as Larry's. Certainly, that driver hadn't made things any easier for her. Still Cassie didn't see why she should be subjected to his impertinence throughout the trip. His attractiveness wasn't to be denied—no way. But he was too damned sure of his appeal and had already come on to her. Well, she wanted no part of him—or any man—

and if she had to fend him off and deal with his sharp-tongued comments, it was going to be a strain. And it might interfere with her work. She'd have to talk to Douglas Tyler about him right away. If the driver had just been hired to bring them here from Nairobi, she would let the matter drop. However, if he was assigned to them for the whole trip he would have to be replaced. Cassie just would insist on it!

Quickly, she got out of the shower and toweled herself dry. She was glad she'd had her hair cut in a wash-and-wear style. Because of that it would only take her a few minutes to put herself together, and then she could hurry to Doug's and get this over with.

She went back into her room and opened her suitcase. For a moment, she had the uncomfortable sensation she'd gotten someone else's bag. Then she remembered that things weren't the way she usually left them because Monica and the driver had packed for her. A surge of anger went through her as she remembered how the man had taunted her. She'd show him he couldn't get away with it! Her mouth was set in a determined line as she began to get ready.

It took her a while to find the things she needed. Finally she pulled out a white polo shirt and slacks. She put them on and slipped some elegant white sandals on her feet, then dabbed on a little makeup. Sure she was looking more than just presentable, she set out to find Doug.

He didn't answer her knock. Spotting Monica and Kate sitting by the pool, Cassie hurried over to them.

"How's the water?" she asked as she approached.

"I feel like I've died and gone to heaven," said Monica. "You coming in?"

"Maybe, after I talk to Doug. Have you seen him?"

"I think he's in the bar," Kate said.

"Thanks," Cassie said, and she turned to go.

"How come you want him?" Monica asked lightly.

Cassie froze for a moment, but quickly reasoned that there was no need to hide what she was doing. "I wanted to ask him to get another driver. I think the one we have is a little too arrogant."

Monica shrugged. "I thought he was kind of cute, but if you don't get along with him, may as well give him the old boot."

"Sure, why not?" Kate chimed in. "I didn't think he was all that great."

"I'm glad you guys are on my side," said Cassie, smiling with relief. "I just hope Doug feels the same way."

"He will," Monica asserted. "He's a pussycat."

Cassie raised her eyebrows. She knew that there was definitely one thing that Douglas Tyler was not and that was a pussycat! Nevertheless, she hoped she might persuade him to see eye to eye with her on this matter of the driver.

With a wave at the models Cassie headed for the bar. It was an especially large thatched hut at the far side of the main building. As she walked through the entrance, she spotted Doug right away. To her amazement she saw the driver sitting at the same table. Almost at the same moment, he saw her, too.

"Well," his deep voice rang out, "if it isn't Ms. Dearborn. I suppose you've come to take me up on my drink offer."

Chapter Two

It was too late to back out now, so Cassie walked resolutely to the table. She looked the driver right in the eye. "Actually I didn't expect to see you here at all. I was looking for Doug," she said.

Then she deliberately turned away from him to face Doug, and was about to ask for a word in private when the driver spoke again. "I suppose you're not surprised to see someone of my disreputable character imbibing the evil grape."

Looking back, she saw him raise his glass of champagne to her in a mocking toast and down it.

He went on cheerfully: "Really, my dear, you should join us in a glass of bubbly. It might sweeten your temper and you might be a lot more pleasing if you were a little more disreputable yourself."

Cassie looked at him coldly. "I have no desire to please you at all. You're the one who should be thinking about pleasing me."

"Ah!" said the driver, with a twinkle in those cold blue eyes. "So that's where my technique went wrong! I knew I must be off somewhere, but I haven't had much experience with you puritanical Yankee women."

"At the rate you're going you're not likely to get much, buster," Cassie shot back.

Throwing his head back, the driver laughed.

As far as Cassie was concerned the man's insolence had gone too far and she didn't care if he knew how she felt. She'd planned to discuss the situation with Douglas privately in order to spare the man's feelings. But now she was willing to let him know exactly what she thought of him. She caught Doug's eye and pointed at the driver, "How long are you going to let this situation go on?"

Doug knew exactly what she was talking about and it seemed to make him uncomfortable. He squirmed a little in his chair, "I don't know. I was kind of enjoying the side show."

"Well, I'm not," Cassie said. "What's the story with him?"

Uneasily, Doug looked over at Jack. "The story?"

"Is it just a one shot deal or is he going to be around for a while?" she demanded.

Pouring himself another glass of champagne, the driver looked at her whimsically. "My dear, I was merely flirting with you a little. I'm not prepared to make any long-term commitments."

Ignoring him, Cassie kept her attention on Doug. "You know what I'm talking about."

Douglas just looked at her blankly. "I thought I did, but I'm lost now."

Cassie tried to keep her temper in cheek. "I want to know how long that man is going to be our driver."

"You think he's our driver?" Doug asked incredulously.

"I should think that would be patently obvious. Why else would she try to ply me with tips?" Jack asked.

It was Cassie's turn to look blank.

Doug started to laugh uproariously. Jack sat calmly sipping his champagne. Leaning over, Doug slapped him on the shoulder, "Don't you think that's hilarious?"

"I had my chuckle over it long ago," Jack said with a polite smile.

This remark sobered Doug. He dried his tears of laughter with a cocktail napkin. Then he started guffawing all over again.

Cassie was getting really annoyed. "What is this?" she asked finally.

"I'm sorry," Doug said. This time he really pulled himself together. Turning to Cassie he nodded formally. "Ms. Cassandra Dearborn, allow me to present Mr. Jonathan Barton-Hyde, one of the foremost authorities on East Africa and owner of the Hillside Resort."

"And the coffee plantation and the game reserve," chimed in Jonathan.

"Right," Doug said.

Cassie just stood there with her mouth hanging open.

"Yes, I suppose I am a real great white hunter. No, I am not of the variety that goes about shooting elephants in their pajamas. And yes, I will be happy to kiss your hand and make all the necessary obeisances, if you really want to go through that particular rite," Jonathan informed her.

On reflex, Cassie clutched her hands together, just in case he really would try to kiss them. "Good gravy," she muttered.

"Aptly put," said Jonathan. "Now perhaps you'd like to continue with your complaints."

"I'd be happy to," she replied. "But I think you just trumped my ace, Jonathan."

"Yes, I did. Didn't I?" he said with a smile. "Incidentally, call me Jack. Even my enemies do. It makes things so much simpler. Now go on. If you have any guts at all you'll tell me what a scoundrel I am."

Cassie's temper flared again. "That's just what I mean. You're always making little digs at me. Saying things about me not having any guts. Why the hell should I be subjected to that impertinence?"

"Perhaps because your reactions amuse me," he countered.

Anxiously, Cassie turned to Doug, "How am I supposed to work if he keeps badgering me like that? Can't you get him out of the way?"

"We need him, Cassie," Doug said.

"He's right, you know," Jack put in. "After all, I am one of the foremost authorities on East Africa. Where as you, Ms. Dearborn, judging from the dossiers your magazine sent me, are a mere novice. I wonder which of us is more expendable?"

"Oh now, I don't think it has to come to that," Doug said. He seemed to be worried that the conflict was getting out of hand.

"Furthermore," said Jack, topping Doug, "I wonder which one of us is in a better position to lose this job. I'm certainly in a very independent situation here at Hillside. Even if your magazine somehow sabotaged my resort business, I'd still have my coffee plantation to fall back on. You, by your own admission, are a recent divorcee. If you didn't have this particular assignment..."

He was hitting below the belt and Cassie wasn't about to let him continue. "I've seen my share of men like you," she blurted out. "You think just because you have a few dollars or shillings or whatever you call money here you can use it to put a shield between yourself and the world. Well, you can damn well go ahead and live that way if you want to, but don't expect me to admire you for it. As far as I'm concerned all you have is worth nothing, nothing at all." Cassie paused to catch her breath. She noticed that the two men were staring at her. Doug seemed truly apprehensive. She spoke to him. "Now it looks like the two of us are going to stuck together on this job. That'll be fine with me as long as

Jack stays well out of my way. If he doesn't, I'm walking."

Cassie stood glaring at the two men, waiting for a reply.

After a moment, Jack shrugged. "I guess the commandant has spoken."

"Precisely," she retorted.

"Well, Ms. Dearborn, you certainly don't encourage anyone to venture into your proximity," he replied.

"Mr. Barton-Hyde," she said. He looked up at her questioningly. "You mentioned earlier today that you were worried about my sense of humor. You'll find it improves enormously once you learn to keep your distance."

With that, Cassie turned and walked out of the bar. She stomped down the path to her room, threw open the door to the small hut and flopped down on the bed.

She was a little surprised, but proud, at the way she'd managed to stand up for herself. Not that she wasn't used to holding her own with men, she'd never been a very passive woman. But she wondered if she would have had the courage to lash out at Jack like that if he hadn't started talking about how rich and powerful he was. Larry had always done that. Cassie had hated that habit and pitied him for it. There had been countless times when Cassie had seen Larry try to buy respect, friendship, and even her love with money. Watching him, Cassie had learned just how worthless dollars could be.

This Jonathan Barton-Hyde was just as bad. He'd expected her to fall at his feet when he told her how much property he owned. Granted, it had been a bit of a shock since he had the manners of a ruffian, not a gentleman. Nevertheless, it didn't give him the right to treat her so rudely.

Cassie rolled over on her side and before she knew it, she'd fallen asleep. She woke about an hour later, realizing that the emotional workout with Jack had taken a lot out of her. She really was going to have to avoid him in the future, for he forced her to stretch to parry his thrusts . . . and that wouldn't leave her with an ounce of energy for her work.

She got out of bed and went to the window. It was early evening; dinner would probably be ready soon. Fighting seemed to give her a tremendous appetite so she went into the bathroom and freshened up a bit. Then she changed into her beige silk lounging slacks and matching camisole—an outfit that Larry had given her. She felt a little funny wearing it since even the thought of him seemed to make her angry lately, but it also seemed silly *not* to wear it. She had to stop making everything connected with Larry into a big emotional issue. With a shrug, she headed outside.

She started up the path to the main building which was where the dining room was, but hadn't gone very far when she heard footsteps behind her.

"Hey, Cassie! Where you going?"

Cassie turned and saw Monica coming down the path after her. Monica was wearing a pair of gold lamé spike heels, red striped pajama bottoms, and a purple T-shirt that said "Sloppy's East Side Eatery" on it. Her hair was in hot rollers and she was carrying a small bottle of nail polish.

"I was checking to see when dinner started."

"Not for another hour yet," Monica said, making a face. "I'm starving. I'm going to get a couple of sodas. Want to come?"

"Okay." Cassie fell into step beside her.

Monica ran a shrewd eye over Cassie's outfit, "You look nice."

"Thanks. I read that people dress for dinner here so I thought what the heck."

"Yeah, I'm going to get all dolled up," Monica said. Then she stopped on the path and held out the bottle of nail polish. "Say, can you get this off?"

"Maybe," replied Cassie as she took the bottle. The plastic cap was all covered with teeth marks. "What in the world have you been doing with this thing? Trying to gnaw it off?"

"Listen, I was getting desperate. I went to a disco the night before we left New York and I put on this silver goop," said Monica, waving her glitter covered nails in Cassie's face. "Anyway, I was getting on the plane and Douglas takes me aside and says that I have to change my nails pronto. That creepy Jill was supposed to do them for me, but I can't find her."

"She's probably off somewhere with Max."

"You'd think she'd be around when I need her. I mean, what's she getting paid for anyway?"

"She works pretty hard. She deserves a little time off," Cassie said gently. Just then she felt the grip of the bottle cap give. "I got it."

"Hot dog," Monica said, smiling her famous gap tooth smile. "For a minute there I was afraid that Douglas would take one look at my silver nails and give me the axe."

Cassie smiled patiently. Monica and Kate were two of the top models in New York. There was no way that Douglas Tyler would ever fire either of them.

"Say, speaking of Douglas firing people, did you get him to dump that chauffeur guy?"

"No such luck," Cassie said wryly, adding quickly, "That driver turned out to be none other than Jonathan Barton-Hyde."

"Whoop-de-doo. What's that got to do with the price of beans in China?" Monica said, staring into the nail polish bottle.

"Jonathan Barton-Hyde is a highly qualified East African expert. Apparently, he's been hired to be our guide."

"Gee, that's too bad, but what can you do?"

"Not much. He seems to be set up in a very powerful position. He owns all this."

Monica put her hand over her mouth and her eyes went wide with excitement, "Oh my stars! He must be as rich as Rockefeller!"

"Well, he seems to think he is, in any case."

"I can't believe it. Here I was in that room with him all that time, you know, packing up your clothes and I didn't even know!"

"Know what?"

"That he was a big important guy."

"He's a little too impressed with his own importance if you ask me," Cassie said.

Monica didn't seem to have heard Cassie's comment. She looked like she was absorbed in her own thoughts.

"Gee," muttered Monica, "And he's nice and tall, too."

Cassie was beginning to follow the direction of Monica's thinking. Monica stood just under six feet. The few times Cassie had ever seen her socially she'd been with very tall, very wealthy men.

"How much does he own? Does he really own *all* this stuff?"

"I think so."

"All by himself?"

"I don't know. Why?"

"Nothing," Monica said. Cassie could tell that she was trying to sound casual. "I just was thinking that it must be a huge responsibility."

"I suppose so," Cassie said, repressing a smile.

"Listen, I gotta go get ready for dinner," said Monica. She was already heading off toward her room.

"I thought we were going to get a soda."

"I can't. I have to get dressed." With that Monica ran off as fast as her spike heels could carry her.

Cassie wanted to laugh. She was sure Monica thought she was being very subtle about the whole thing. However, she'd made it perfectly clear that she had her eye out for a wealthy man—and a tall one best of all. For a second, Cassie was tempted to go after Monica and tell her what insufferable pigs rich men could be and she should steer clear of Jack.

Suddenly another thought hit her: Jack and Monica might actually get along. If Jack were looking to catch an attractive woman, he couldn't find anyone more beautiful than Monica. And Monica certainly seemed eager to be caught.

Cassie sighed. It seemed so strange to see someone running full speed into a situation that she'd just gotten out of. How painful it was when a woman made the wrong choice in a man. Perhaps, though, Monica would never know that kind of suffering.

Squaring her shoulders, Cassie decided to put all that out of her mind. She was in one of the most beautiful places she'd ever seen in her life and she was determined to enjoy it. The sun was setting and the muted light softened the colors of the riotously bright flowers. The hills around her rolled off in every direction. The jacaranda trees swayed gently in the wind. She felt calm for the first time since she'd left New York, maybe peaceful was an even better word. She sat down in one of the wicker garden chairs and drew her legs up against her chest. She put her head down on her knees and smiled to herself.

At first, she heard the sound only faintly and she couldn't tell what it was. Then it became more distinct and she realized that someone was whistling. But it wasn't just an ordinary little tune, it was a sad, powerfully haunting sound. She lifted her head and listened. Each trembling note had a yearning quality to it that seemed to reflect the way she herself felt. It was an odd mixture of emotions. There was some sadness and loneliness, yet there was also a contented self-sufficiency.

Cassie wondered who was making the sound. Certainly Barry didn't have the kind of soul one would need to whistle so plaintively. Douglas Tyler was tone deaf, so it couldn't be he.

Just then, Jonathan Barton-Hyde stepped out from behind an oleander hedge and turned down the path in front of her chair. His mouth was puckered and he was whistling that lovely melody. Cassie didn't move. He took another step and then he saw her. The whistle quickly changed into a low expletive sound, and then died.

She rose and they stood staring at each other for a long moment. Jack started to say something, but stopped himself and walked away. Cassie had the strangest feeling that he was running from her.

When she walked into the dining room, Cassie stopped in her tracks. It was beautifully designed to make the most of its location. The east and west walls were windows that allowed a view of both sunrise and sunset. The ceiling was very high, with exposed wood beams, and the decor was based on African motifs. The sculptures were especially striking and seemed to have been selected for their simple elegance.

Cassie saw Douglas Tyler sitting by himself so she hurried to his table. "Doug, do you think we could shoot a couple of sessions here?" she asked.

Looking up from the piece of papaya he was eating, Doug frowned. "We have to talk."

Cassie felt her throat tighten. She knew she'd caused him plenty of problems today and this probably wasn't the best time to have chosen to start making requests. Quickly, she sat down in the chair next to his. "Look," she began, "I know I messed up something awful coming in late before. Honestly, it won't happen once we start to shoot."

"I'm not worried about that," Doug said with a wave of his fork.

"Mr. Barton-Hyde?"

"I just don't want you two at each other's throats. I've got enough on my mind as it is."

"Fine," Cassie said firmly. "I'll be happy to stay away from him."

Doug studied her for a moment. "You sure about that? No hidden plans for revenge or anything?"

Cassie shook her head. "I'm a little disappointed in you, Doug. I thought you knew I didn't operate that way."

"I agree that it isn't your usual style. But then, neither is showing up late and neither is getting into a cat and dog fight with some stranger in front of the whole crew."

"I promise I won't do it again," said Cassie. "As long as you promise to call off the dog."

"He's a decent guy, a damned decent guy. He'll leave you alone."

Cassie certainly didn't agree with the decent guy part, but she was trying to make peace with Doug so she wasn't about to contradict him.

Doug looked Cassie over thoughtfully. "Something's bothering you, isn't it?"

Shrugging, she tried to act casual. "Nothing a few weeks in Africa won't cure."

Cassie hadn't realized her anxiety was that apparent. She knew she didn't trust Doug enough to let him see her vulnerabilities. But, he was looking at her earnestly, as though he really expected to talk about them.

Just then a waiter arrived and Cassie was saved from

the awkward situation. He held a tray out for her that was piled high with papayas, mangoes, pineapples, and other tropical fruits. Everything was fresh and running with juice.

"Would Madame care for some fruits?" the waiter asked with a formal nod.

"Oh, yes, those are all my favorites," she said as she piled her plate high with fruit. "Thanks so much."

The waiter left and Cassie turned back to Doug with a grin. "I think I'll just make a meal of this. I haven't had such wonderful looking fruit since I used to go to Hawaii."

"With Larry?" Doug asked gently.

Irritated, Cassie looked Doug square in the face. She wished he wouldn't bring up Larry's name. Doug really should be sensitive enough to know that she didn't want to talk about him. However, she wasn't about to cause a scene over it. She'd given Doug enough trouble today already.

"Yeah, the good old days and all that," Cassie said coolly.

"You're upset over the divorce, aren't you?"

"I don't know," she answered curtly. "A person just picks up and goes on, right?"

"Is it really that simple?"

"What are you getting at, Doug?"

Suddenly, Doug looked very vulnerable. Cassie had never seen a hint of such an emotion on his face before and it threw her off balance.

"Did you know Ellie and I are separated?" he asked. He looked down at the table as he spoke, as if he were trying to hide his emotion.

"I'm sorry," Cassie mumbled. She felt like a real fool. Here she'd thought Doug was trying to pry into her personal life when all the poor man was doing was looking for an opening to talk about his own problems. Instinctively, she reached out and put her hand over his. He covered her hand with his free one and they just sat there for a moment. Finally Cassie spoke again, "What a time for you to be going away, huh?"

"It's the best thing I can do," he said. "A distraction."

Cassie nodded. "For me, too."

"Both on the rebound, aren't we?" He looked up at her with a very serious expression.

She wasn't quite sure when he meant. Yet she knew she suddenly felt very uncomfortable looking into his eyes with her hand imprisoned by his. "Maybe things will still work out between you and Ellie. There's time."

"I don't really want them to," Doug said simply. "But it's sweet of you to say that."

Cassie pulled her hand away from his grasp. She didn't want to talk about this any more. The whole conversation was becoming much too personal and she wanted to keep things between her and Doug very, very businesslike.

"I don't know what it was exactly," he continued. "Nothing was happening between us. It had been that way for some time."

Nervously, Cassie started pushing her fruit around on her plate. "Do you mind if we don't go into this?" She fished for an excuse to get out of the conversation. "It's just hard for me to talk about this sort of thing right now. You can understand, can't you?"

Doug looked a little disappointed, but he nodded his agreement. "Maybe we should just bury ourselves in our work and all that," he said, with a teasing twinkle in his eye.

Cassie laughed, partly because she was glad to see him cheering up and partly because she was glad to be out of the sticky conversation. "Sounds good to me," she said. "What about my suggestion for using this room? I think it would be the perfect spot to shoot the resort evening wear. The girls could pose near those sculptures with the garden in the background."

Doug set his silverware down and stared over Cassie's shoulder at the doorway. "Lord in heaven," he muttered.

"What?" Cassie asked.

Doug nodded toward the doorway. "Now I know why I'm paying her so much money."

Turning to look, Cassie saw Monica standing in the doorway, using it as a perfect frame for her body. It was the kind of dramatic entrance that only a born model knows how to make. Monica looked just like a princess, with her brunette hair swept up on top of her head in a regal style and her dress a plain white evening gown with an absolutely beautiful cut. Even on the covers of the best fashion magazines, Monica had never looked more exquisite.

Coming forward a few steps, she struck another pose. Her pale blue eyes scanned the faces in the room, then registered disappointment. Whoever she had made the entrance for didn't seem to be here. Quickly, Monica recovered and strode toward Doug and Cassie.

"Greetings, greetings," she said as she sat down. "What's up?"

"You've just won a point for Cassandra," Doug said.

"Me?"

"She was just asking if we could shoot evening resort wear in here. I'm officially giving her the go ahead right now after that entrance of yours." Doug grinned at them both.

Quickly, Cassie swallowed the piece of mango she was eating and dabbed her napkin to her mouth. Finally she could speak. "Doug, that's terrific! You're not going to believe how good it's going to look!"

"Monica's little preview proved that I'm bound to like the rest." Then he gestured toward the entrance. "There's Jack now. I just realized I ought to check with him before we start making too many plans."

Monica brightened. "I'll go get him," she said eagerly.

Before Cassie could stop her, Monica was up and sweeping toward Jack. Cassie couldn't help admiring her. Monica really knew how to carry herself—the tilt of her head, the angle at which she held her hands, everything was perfect. Cassie looked over at Jack to see how he was responding. To her surprise, he was looking Monica over with a hard, very calculating stare. There was something frightening in his expression. Cassie thought he looked like the kind of man who could use a woman for his own pleasure and then roughly push her aside without another thought. It surprised her that she'd ever believed she'd seen gentleness in his face. Obviously, she'd been mistaken.

As Cassie watched, Monica walked right up to him. He put his hands on her bare shoulders. Monica gave him a shy, thoroughly provocative smile and ran one of her fingers along his shoulder and forearm.

"Now there's an attractive couple," Doug said. "I'd ask Jack to model for us, if I didn't think he might be insulted."

"Spare me the hassle of photographing him, please," Cassie said.

Monica slipped her arm through Jack's and led him to their table. She was laughing at something he'd said. As they sat down, she reached up and tugged at one of his thick, dark curls. "You know, you need a haircut, don't you think?"

"I suppose you'd like it clipped into some neat and orderly design like Doug's here," Jack said, grinning amiably.

"Sure, his is pretty cute," Monica said on a lightly teasing note.

"Then I promise to give the matter some thought," Jack said. He looked at Cassie and smiled.

She dropped her gaze to her plate, speared the last piece of fruit, ate it, then pushed her plate aside and stood up.

"I'm going to go now. See you all tomorrow," she said.

Jack smirked at her. "Ms. Dearborn, I hope my presence isn't driving you away. I'd hate to have you miss a meal on my account."

"You flatter yourself if you think you have the power to send me running," Cassie said levelly. "The fact is I have to get up early tomorrow for work." With that she turned and marched out of the dining room.

As she walked back to her room, Cassie felt much more confident than she had earlier. She had had a good solid idea for her photography which made her feel much more secure about her job. Also, that irritating situation with Jack seemed to be more under control.

In her room she paced for a while before changing into her nightgown. She wasn't really tired yet, so she decided to read in bed until she fell asleep. There were a couple of paperbacks in her suitcase. Also, she'd noticed before that the hotel had provided a book that appeared interesting. It was called "How to Recognize the Wild Animals of Kenya."

She picked it up from the bedside table and opened the cover. Someone had written inside, in red marker, "Girls—the only really *wild* animal in this country is Mr. Jonathan Barton-Hyde." Cassie slammed the book shut. The anxiety came back in a rush as she realized what had been bothering her about Jack all along. Every instinct told her he was just a shallow ladies' man. Handsome, self-assured, sexy—just the kind of man who inspired love and never gave it. And this bit of graffiti in the book was the clincher.

Cassie padded restlessly around the hut. She hated men like that. Hated them. Womanizing was the one thing about Larry that she could never forgive. He'd insisted on his right to sleep with other women even though he was married to her. She was supposed to "understand." He wasn't the least dissatisfied with her, but he needed fresh conquests from time to time to support his sense of tough masculinity. So women were "supports"—objects—to him... and hadn't there been something of that same ruthlessness with women in Jack's eyes as he'd looked at Monica? Oh, yes! Cassie felt a scorching loathing for Jack. Monica was welcome to him.

Chapter Three

THE SUN WAS just beginning to rise on this first day of actual shooting and Cassie was eager to immerse herself in her photography. She'd insisted on getting an early start to catch the morning light. They would rest at noon because the harsh overhead light cast unflattering shadows on the models' faces, and if there were any shots Cassie still needed she could take them later in the softer afternoon light.

She liked to wear sensible, comfortable clothes for photo sessions and so dressed this morning in a pair of designer jeans, a short sleeved khaki shirt, and sneakers. It was a workmanlike outfit. Nothing else would do. There were too many times when she had to lie flat on her stomach or climb up on a precarious perch in order to get the right angle.

Passing Barry's hut, she saw through the open door that the models were already inside. They had their hair in hot rollers and Barry was starting to do Kate's makeup. Doug, too, was there hurrying everything along. When he saw Cassie he waved and came running out.

"I'm going to send you and Max on ahead," he told her.

"Sure," she agreed.

"That way you can start planning out your shots and we'll be ready to go when the models get there. I figure we'll save at least twenty minutes this way."

"Fine," Cassie said, noticing that Doug was getting

that demonic look in his eye that he always got when work needed to be done. She smiled at him.

"I've sent Max and Jill over to get Jonathan. They should be out front any minute."

"I'll be there waiting for them. You don't need to worry about a thing," Cassie said soothingly.

"I knew I could count on you," Doug said, and patted her on the fanny.

Cassie tensed, but Doug didn't even seem to notice her reaction. He just turned and headed back into Barry's hut. She stood looking after him. She boiled when a man did such a thing. It was demeaning, especially in a professional situation. In this case, too, the gesture could be just another one of those fashion industry customs that she found so phony. Cassie shrugged and started walking toward the front drive.

Just as she got there Jack's jeep pulled up. As was to be expected, Max and Jill were snuggling in the back, which left Cassie the seat next to Jack. She gritted her teeth.

"Hi, you guys," she said as she climbed up into the seat.

"Morning, Cassie," said Max.

"Isn't it a great day?" Jill asked as she leaned against Max's shoulder.

"Yes, it is. It's nice here," Cassie replied.

Jack turned to her and smiled. "Don't I get a good morning?"

"No," she said as she pointedly turned away from him. Cassie couldn't see his reaction but if he was angry it didn't really show in his driving. He started the jeep smoothly and drove out of the resort area.

He headed down the main road for a while, then turned off on a narrow one-lane track, following it for only about twenty yards before he stopped. Cassie turned in alarm.

"Why are we stopping?" she asked.

"I just wanted to warn you not to talk," Jack said as he angled himself around so that he could see Max and Jill, too.

"What's the problem?" Max asked, putting a protective arm around Jill.

"No problem," Jack replied. "But if you want to see some wildlife you'll have to be quiet or you'll scare the animals away."

"Okay," Jill whispered.

Jack drove on. The country they were going through was partly forest, partly grasslands. Cassie didn't see anything but brush and trees for the next five minutes and was beginning to get bored with looking for wildlife when Jack stopped the jeep again. There on the road in front of them were three of the ugliest animals she had ever seen.

"What the hell are those?" Jill asked softly.

"Warthogs," Jack hissed.

Cassie couldn't help thinking about how perfect the name was. They looked like a sort of wild boar, but their bodies were scrawnier and their tusks larger. They looked very ungainly and she wondered how they could move gracefully at all with those huge tusks protruding from their snouts.

"Shall we go on?" Jack asked.

"I suppose," Max said reluctantly.

"Don't worry," Jack said. "You'll see plenty of these at the observation post. It's just nice to get a good close look."

He slowly edged the jeep forward. The warthogs glared at the approaching vehicle, then calmly ambled out of the way.

"They seem so tame," Cassie said. "Why do we have to be quiet?"

Jack was studying her, but Cassie thought she noticed

a slight smile of satisfaction playing at the corners of his lips. So he was pleased she'd initiated conversation, was he? "Mind answering my question?" she asked tartly.

"Not at all, not at all. Delighted to, in fact. Those warthogs are hardly tame," he said. "You'd realize that soon enough if you ever got out of the jeep around here."

"They wouldn't attack, would they?" Max asked as he tightened his protective grip on Jill.

"Probably not unless they felt threatened themselves," Jack replied. "But you never can tell how a wild creature will react."

"But we're safe in the jeep?" Jill asked a little nervously.

"Reasonably," Jack said. "It always pays to be cautious around certain animals. I try to stay a nice safe distance away from elephants and rhinos. When you see animals in the bush, it's important to see them on their own terms. If you know a creature doesn't like to be crowded you have to give it some distance. If you know the animals are disturbed by loud noise and fast-moving vehicles, then talk quietly and drive slowly."

"Sounds reasonable," Max said.

"Yes," Jack said. "A person can get on very well out here with a little common sense. Don't you agree, Ms. Dearborn?"

Cassie started a little and glanced at him. He was looking at her with that odd smile of his. His expression made her uneasy. "Dear me," she said archly, "I *did* think we were supposed to be observing a vow of silence. No point in scaring the animals and all that, right?"

Jack chuckled a little. "Right, Ms. Dearborn. We'll hold discussion until we get inside the observation post."

They drove on in silence until they reached the wildlife observation post for the Hillside Resort. The post was on the roof of a deserted homestead, which had been built by European settlers. Nearby was a waterhole. Visitors to Hillside could spend the day in the observation post watching the wild animals come to drink.

Jack put his finger to his lips as a signal for them to remain quiet before he got out of the jeep and came around to open the door. They had to walk about a hundred yards across a grassy field in order to get to the observation post. Cassie saw Jack take a gun out of the back of the jeep. He held it in readiness as he escorted them to the entrance ladder. Jill huddled close to Max. Cassie felt wary crossing alone, but she wasn't about to appeal to Max—let alone Jack for heaven's sake—for protection.

They reached the ladder to the observation area and Jill went first. Max motioned for Cassie to follow, but she shook her head and nodded for him to go on.

As Cassie climbed up, she was acutely aware of Jack behind her and wished she'd allowed Max his bit of chivalry. But such thoughts vanished at the sight of the interior of the observation post. She couldn't believe how lovely and modern it was. It was all wood and glass, every inch in the style of the main building at the resort. The furnishings were simple, yet comfortable looking, and the decor had the same African motifs and batik fabrics. Through the large windows she could see the surrounding field and the waterhole. Off to one side was the outdoor observation deck. Cassie peered at it through the glass door. She intended to do most of her shooting out there.

"I hope you can do all your planning work back here in the lounge area," Jack said. "Don't want to frighten off the animals before we begin."

"I suppose we can manage," Cassie said.

"Besides," he added, "baboons climb up on the deck. They can be a bit difficult to cope with if you're not used to them."

"We'll stay inside," Jill said quickly.

"I'm going back to get the others then," Jack said.

With that, he climbed down the ladder, closing the trap door entrance behind him. Max and Cassie immediately started planning the shots. They discussed what different props from the deck and lounge area they would like to use. Jill made notes on everything so that nothing would be forgotten.

Cassie could scarcely believe how quickly the time had flown when she heard the faint sound of the bus's motor. Looking out the window, she saw Jack pull up and park again. Kate, Monica, Doug, and Barry had been joined by two of the men who worked for Jack, who were carrying big boxes that looked like they were full of food and wine.

As the group crossed the field, Cassie noticed that Monica took Jack's arm. When they came closer, she saw Monica look intently at him, then toss her fine dark hair back with her fingers. It was one of her more effective poses and, Cassie noticed, it seemed to have some effect on Jack. He actually took his watchful eyes off the surrounding field and looked at Monica with surprise.

They all climbed up into the observation post lounge, and immediately the two men servants started making coffee and setting out trays full of pastries and tropical fruit. Doug paced the room rapidly, then clapped his hands together a couple of times.

"You ready?" he asked, looking anxiously at Cassie and Max.

Cassie nodded.

"Let's get out there and get cracking then," Doug said.

"Hey," Jack said, "Hold on a minute."

Doug turned and glared at him irritably.

"Let me just give you a quick rundown on the ground rules before you get to work," Jack continued.

Doug glanced uneasily at his watch. "Okay. Okay."

Jack nodded at Doug curtly. He didn't seem to like the way Doug was pressuring everyone to get to work. "First of all," he began, "the really important thing to remember is that you have to stay quiet. Talking in low voices is fine, however loud noises, laughter, and so forth will frighten the animals away from the waterhole. It may take them up to several hours to return so you won't have full advantage of your location. Running on the outdoor deck is also prohibited. Again for the same reason. If you follow these simple rules everything should go very well for you here. Any questions?"

Before anyone had a chance to ask anything, Doug clapped his hands together again. "Okay, everybody! Let's go."

The models moved toward the door to the deck. Cassie gathered up her equipment case. Max picked up the props for the first series of shots.

"One more thing," said Jonathan.

Everyone stopped. Doug turned back to him with an exasperated expression.

"Watch out for the baboons," Jack said.

"What?" Monica asked, her nose charmingly wrinkling to show bewilderment.

"The baboons here sometimes climb to the deck. They look almost friendly but they are wild creatures and one must never make the mistake of thinking they're pets."

"All right," Doug said. "Everybody watch out. Let's go now."

The group filed out onto the deck. Max set an African sculpture that they'd planned to use in one corner. Cassie took the two models aside.

"Okay, you guys," she said, "here's the situation. I want to get a series of you lounging around over in that corner where Max is."

"Sitting on the railing?" Kate suggested. "How would that be?"

"Fine," Cassie said. "I'm going to get up on that table so I can get an angle down onto the waterhole."

Monica looked at the railing doubtfully. "I'm not going to get splinters sitting on that am I?"

Just then a huge baboon appeared on the railing. The women all gasped.

"He's disgusting!" Monica said.

"I think he's kind of sweet," countered Cassie.

"How can you even say that!" Monica cried. "Look at him!"

As the girls watched, the baboon climbed up on top of the deck railing and paraded back and forth. When the animal walked away from them, Cassie noticed there was a perfect circle of bare pink flesh right in the middle of its buttocks.

Monica nudged Cassie. "See what I mean. He doesn't have any hair on his fanny. He's hideous!"

"'He' is a she," drawled a deep masculine voice. Cassie whipped her head around. Jack was standing just behind her. She stiffened a little and took a half step away. Jack continued, "We call her Agnes. She's the boldest of the baboons."

"That sounds like a rather dubious distinction," Cassie said irritably.

Jack turned to her with a grin. "Dubious or not. That's exactly what Agnes is. She'll steal anything that's not nailed down. That includes your camera equipment, Ms. Dearborn. So if I were you, my sweet, I would thank me for the warning."

"I don't need you to tell me how to do my job," Cassie flared. "I'm perfectly capable of looking out for my equipment myself."

"I stand corrected," Jack said coldly.

Just then Kate nudged Cassie and nodded toward

Doug. He was staring at the group impatiently. Cassie knew she'd better get right down to business or Doug would start rushing her through her work.

She turned back to Jack. Why did he make her so damned edgy? She should be able to freeze him out. "You know, we do have a job to do," she snapped, "if you don't mind."

His cold blue eyes darkened with anger and he turned to leave.

"Hey, Jack," Monica called after him. "Thanks for telling us about the cute little animals."

"My pleasure," said Jack as he walked away.

"Why don't you go get settled?" said Cassie to the models.

As Monica and Kate went over to the corner where they were supposed to work, Cassie picked up her equipment case and carried it back inside. When she passed Jack, she saw him raise an eyebrow. She knew he was thinking that she wouldn't have been so cautious if he hadn't warned her about the baboon. It was true. She probably wouldn't have been. However, she would never admit that to Jack. She didn't want to be indebted to him for anything.

She hurried over to where the girls were and checked her light meter. Then she climbed up on the table and adjusted the lens focus. While she was doing that Barry examined the model's faces to make sure that their hair and makeup were perfect.

"Everything okay?" asked Cassie.

"Take off," said Barry as he stepped out of the way.

Cassie had noticed before that there was a family of warthogs drinking and resting by the waterhole. She angled her camera so that she could include the animals in her shot. She grinned. It was perfect. The sculpture and the animals in the background gave the ideal African effect.

Skillfully, the models fell into their poses. They'd both been working at this for so long that they instinctively kept their hands and faces at the correct angles. Cassie rarely had to direct them. That was fortunate because she didn't want to frighten the animals out of the range of her camera.

The clothes they were wearing looked just right. Kate had on a khaki safari shorts outfit which brought out the tawny highlights in her thick red hair. Monica was in white. Her clothes made her fine brunette hair look almost jet black. Cassie knew she was getting some great shots. She felt more and more confident as she realized that this was a series of shots that were just right for the magazine.

Finally, after an hour and a half, Cassie signaled for a break. The models went into the lounge to change for the next shot and Cassie sat down on the table with a sigh. It had been an exhausting session, but a gratifying one.

"For you!"

Cassie turned around slowly and looked Jack in the eye. "What now?"

He held a coffee cup out to her. Cassie merely stared at it.

"I could have gotten my own."

"I'm sure you could. I just thought this might be appreciated." He paused. "Ah, that's it!" he said.

"What is?" Cassie asked levelly.

"I see the lights of anger truly are on now in those lovely eyes."

"I'm not that angry."

"Yes, you are. You're just hiding it well."

"I suppose you think it's funny."

Jonathan smiled that odd smile. It made goosebumps rise on Cassie's skin. "Actually, I do find all this a bit amusing," he said.

"Well, I don't," she said. "I have a job to do and you seem to be determined to irritate me while I'm trying to do it."

"Not at all. I'm sure you can use a pick-me-up after all that work, and that's why I brought you the coffee."

She ground out a "thank you" and snatched the cup from his hand. The movement, motivated by her profound annoyance with the man, was too jerky and forceful. The coffee rocketed out of the cup in a huge arc over her shoulder.

"Hey! Hey! What do you think you're doing?" cried Barry.

Cassie spun around and saw that the coffee was all over the front of Barry's jeans.

"Oh no," she muttered.

She jumped off the table and raced to Barry. "I'm so sorry. It was an accident. Honest."

"That's beside the point, don't you think? These are my best jeans and I'm thousands of miles away from my favorite dry cleaner."

Poor Barry looked so foolish as he tried to clean off his jeans with a paper napkin. Jack's barely suppressed chuckles reached Cassie's ears, tempting her to laugh, too.

"Look, Barry. If they're ruined I'll get you a new pair when we get back to New York. I promise."

"It's certainly the least you can do," Barry said.

"Please," Jack said. "Let my servants take care of it."

"No," Cassie said quickly.

"Why not?" he asked calmly. Any trace of amusement he still might have felt was masked behind an extraordinarily polite expression.

"They won't shrink these, will they?" Barry asked.

"Of course not," Jack replied.

Cassie scowled. "Don't worry, Barry," she said, "I'll take care of it back in the city."

"There's really no need," Jack countered. "It's easily taken care of here."

"But I said I'd do it," flared Cassie.

"Please, keep your voice down, Ms. Dearborn," said Jack.

Clamping her mouth shut, Cassie glanced at the animals by the waterhole. The talking didn't seem to be upsetting them at all. She guessed that Jack must be using this whole thing about disturbing the animals as some sort of power game. She turned back to him. "Why don't you just mind your own business?"

"I believe the matter at hand is Barry's business," said Jack coolly. Then he looked over at Barry. "Shall I have them fix your pants?"

"Okay," said Barry. "May as well. I'd hate to be without these jeans for the whole trip."

"I'm going inside," said Cassie. She stomped off into the lounge.

Once indoors she fixed herself another cup of coffee, selected a Danish pastry, took her food to a chair by the window, and sat down. As she nibbled at the edge of the pastry, she stared out at the meadow and the line of trees that bordered it. The wind was blowing gently through the leaves and parting the grass. Everything looked so beautiful. She really did like Africa. Also, her work had gone so well this morning that she couldn't feel less than elated by it.

The only problem was Jack...and the overly emotional responses she had toward him. The way he nettled her was all out of proportion and undermined her confidence. She grimaced. As a professional photographer she had to be able to handle all sorts of difficult people with cool poise—a point on which she was fouling up totally with Jonathan Barton-Hyde. Cassie resolved to work out this problem, which gave the lie to her sense of maturity as well as her professionalism. She was startled out of her reflections by a hissed sentence.

"Quick! There are giraffes! Hurry!"

Cassie looked up, startled. Doug was standing next to her with a khaki sun hat in his hands that he was wringing into knots.

"What?" she asked.

"There are giraffes!"

"Where?"

"Over by the trees on the far side," he said rapidly. "If you hurry you can get them in the background for that next series of shots."

"Okay, let's go," said Cassie as she stood up. "Are the models ready?"

"Barry has to retouch their makeup and hair. Other than that they're fine."

"Terrific," she replied. "I'll meet them outside."

Cassie hurried to see the giraffes and knew they'd make an excellent background for the next shots. She quickly checked the light meter reading. Deciding to use her second camera, she took off the lens cap and put it in the back pocket of her jeans. Then she adjusted her focus. She was ready to go as soon as the models were.

Looking around for Kate and Monica, Cassie saw Jack leaning against the door of the lounge. His arms were folded across his hard, muscular chest and he was watching her with a haughty expression. Cassie looked back at him coolly just as the lounge door opened, throwing him a little off balance. However, Jack seemed not to notice the smirk on Cassie's face. He was looking at Kate and Monica as they came out of the lounge wearing slacks. Kate was in blue. Monica was in purple.

"What do you think?" asked Monica as she turned to show off the garments for Jack.

"Perfection." Jack smiled.

"Gee, thanks," Monica said.

Barry and Doug came rushing out of the lounge. Barry

stopped and glared at Cassie. Doug pushed the models toward the spot where they were supposed to pose.

"Let's go. Let's go," Doug muttered.

"Come on, Doug," Monica said. "Keep your shirt on."

Cassie could see Doug's neck reddening. He obviously wanted to make some sort of outburst but he restrained himself. "Let's just get down to business, Monica."

The model shrugged and took her place. Lord, Cassie thought, Doug had to be one of the most driven human beings she'd ever encountered. She forced herself to concentrate on the models and soon was totally absorbed with their imagery and that of the truly magnificent giraffes in the distance.

"That's great, gals," Cassie said quietly as Kate and Monica started fooling around with some really funny poses. How she liked the look of these shots! The poses seemed to emphasize that this sportswear was for zesty, active people. As Cassie continued to work, she thought she felt somebody poking at her to try to get her attention. She refused to break her concentration at this truly creative moment and absently waved her hand behind her to make the person leave her alone. The next thing Cassie knew she stepped on something that felt like a dog's paw or a child's hand. She heard an animal cry out in pain. She turned around and saw that she was face to face with Agnes the baboon.

The baboon's face seemed panicky and her eyes shifted as though she wanted to run away. But apparently Agnes realized she was cornered up against the lounge building, and turning on Cassie, she displayed an ugly set of teeth.

Letting out a scream, Cassie raced toward the lounge. However, her escape was blocked by Jack's powerful frame. In a panic Cassie slugged him in the chest, trying to get him out of the way so that she could make her escape. Suddenly, she felt herself going up in the air as Jack lifted her off the deck. He was laughing again, laughing at her.

"All right, Agnes," Jack said. "You've made your point."

As he held Cassie aloft, Jack fended the animal off with his bush boots. Agnes retreated a safe distance and began licking one of her handlike paws.

"I hope you didn't hurt her," Jack said as he took a step toward the now subdued animal to see better the extent of the injury. Agnes looked up at them and made threatening motions and sounds, again baring those teeth. "I think she's all right. Lucky you were wearing sneakers or you might have done some real damage. I don't think there would have been much I could have done for her if you'd broken her hand."

"Okay, Atlas," Cassie said as she tried to push herself away from his chest. "You and the baboon have both made your points. You can put me down now."

Jack looked at Cassie, then at Agnes, then back at Cassie. "Do you really think that's wise?"

Quickly, Cassie glanced down at the baboon. Agnes glared at her and bared her teeth. "No, I guess you're right. It's not such a good idea after all."

"I shouldn't think so," Jack replied. "Agnes seems to have taken a fancy to that lens cap you put in your back pocket. She might insist on having it after what you just did to her hand."

"Well, she's out of luck. I need it."

"Then you'd better stay just where you are," Jack said as he adjusted her weight in his arms.

"I've got a better idea," said Cassie.

"What's that?"

"Why don't you just carry me into the lounge and set me down there?"

"Oh now, you can't really expect me to carry you off," Jack said with a slight smirk.

"Hardly what I had in mind when you say it in *that* tone of voice!" Cassie said.

"What a relief," Jack countered, "because you've ruined your chances with any self-respecting great white hunter after that little stunt you just pulled."

"Believe me. It was an accident. I didn't come here to maim the wildlife."

"No, but you did intend to photograph some of the animals. That banshee shriek of yours sent every wild thing for miles around scurrying for cover."

Glancing over at the waterhole, Cassie saw that he was right. The family of warthogs had fled. The giraffes were no longer visible either.

"See what I mean?" said Jack.

"That's another point for you and the baboons," said Cassie. "The animals actually don't like loud noises." Then Cassie noticed that Agnes the baboon was still sitting on the deck watching her. "Except your pal, Agnes, didn't seem to mind my screams. What's she doing here?"

"Waiting for revenge," Jack said dryly. "You'd better be nice to me or I may just let her take it."

Cassie looked nervously at the baboon, then back at Jack. "Please cut the nonsense and get me out of here."

Laughing, Jack held her even tighter. "As I said before you can't expect a great white hunter to carry you off after that little escapade. But then I certainly don't want to leave you to Agnes's mercy." His voice dropped to a husky drawl. "What shall I do with you?"

Excitement stirred in the pit of Cassie's stomach. The question was laden with sexual innuendo and reinforced by a slightly stronger pressure of Jack's arms, forcing her body closer into his. Cassie gulped a quick breath and then one quicker still as she met his gaze. There was no ice in those blue eyes now—none—and they kindled a response deep within her. She blinked to make what surely had to be a fantasy refocus into reality. But her pulses only beat faster. Jack's fingers dug sensuously into her flesh and she felt giddy with a crazy longing to caress him back, to taste his lips.

"I'm going mad," she muttered.

"Hmm—temporary insanity or permanent lunacy, Ms. Dearborn?" he murmured in her ear, his breath stirring a delicious tremor which streaked along her neck and spine.

"I'll take her," Doug said loudly and they both started.

Cassie had forgotten about everyone. The crew had seen her make a fool of herself with the baboon and what was even more embarrassing had overheard her conversation with Jack as well as seeing this little encounter. Quickly, Cassie peeked around and sighed with relief. Max, Jill, and Kate seemed fairly indifferent to all the carrying-on. Barry looked as though he were pleased that she'd finally gotten hers, and only Monica was scowling at her and Jack.

"Let me take her off your hands," Doug repeated.

Jack looked down at Cassie coolly. "Does Ms. Dearborn have any objection to that arrangement?"

Cassie hesitated a moment. She couldn't help remembering last night when she'd reached over to comfort Doug and he'd held her hand just a little bit too long. She didn't want to get into another awkward situation with Doug. Yet, she had to put an end to this ridiculous episode with Jack, who was smiling sardonically at her.

"Just get me out of here," she said to Doug, trying to make it sound like a joke.

Doug reached over and took her out of Jack's arms. Cassie felt Doug stagger a little under her weight and she suddenly felt embarrassingly heavy.

"I'm sorry," she mumbled.

"Forget it," he muttered. His face looked grim with determination as he struggled to carry her into the lounge.

Chapter Four

WITH A STIFLED groan, Doug set Cassie down on a couch by the window and then he sat down next to her. His face was flushed and he was panting slightly from the effort of carrying her in from the observation deck.

Turning around, Doug tried to catch the eye of one of the servants. The couch he and Cassie were sitting on was in the far corner of the lounge, so the man didn't really notice his gestures. Finally Doug leaned over the back of the couch and snapped his fingers.

"Hey, you!" he cried.

The servant looked up in surprise.

"Didn't you see me calling you?" Doug asked irritably.

Cassie cringed. She hated to see people being treated badly just because they happened to work in a serving position.

"No, sir," the man replied politely.

"Well, keep an eye out next item," Doug said. "Bring me a bottle of cold champagne and some of those French cheeses. And make it snappy."

"Immediately, sir."

Doug looked back at Cassie and smiled. "Well?"

"Look," Cassie said. "I don't think you need to worry about the animals being frightened away. I mean, I think we're covered. The stuff this morning went especially well."

Doug didn't say anything for a moment. Cassie felt uncomfortable. It seemed that in every conversation she had with Doug she was apologizing for something. It was annoying to always be on the defensive like that. However, she wanted to assure him that she was a conscientious professional.

Finally Doug said, "I think we'll do a little more after the lunch break. I want to make sure everything's right."

"Then this is the break?"

"Sure."

"Don't you think you'd better tell the others?"

"Had Barry do it."

"Oh." Glancing over her shoulder Cassie noticed that everyone else was milling around at the other end of the lounge. She was alone with Doug in a secluded corner and studied him curiously, wondering if he had purposely contrived this little tête-à-tête.

The servant arrived with the champagne and cheese. He set everything down but the bottle. "Shall I pop the cork, sir?"

Doug nodded. The man opened the champagne and poured it, then moved off as quickly as proper conduct allowed, Cassie thought. Doug held up his glass for a toast and Cassie raised her drink as well.

"You do the honors," he said.

"To one of the most successful magazine issues ever."

"I suppose that will do for a start," Doug said as their glasses clinked. "Now it's my turn."

"Okay," Cassie said, and raised her glass again.

"To one of the most attractive photographers I've ever met," he said with a warm smile.

Nervously, she touched her glass to his. Two men coming on to her one right after the other! What was going on? She decided that the best way to handle the situation was to change the subject as fast as possible.

"The champagne's quite good. I'm glad they can get it down here."

"I don't want to talk about champagne," Doug said. "I want to talk about you."

"What about me?" she asked coolly. "There's not much to tell."

"Where did you grow up?"

"Ohio," she said. Then she added defensively, "Why?"

"You seem like a very elegant woman. I thought you might be one of those Boston bluebloods."

"Hardly," said Cassie. "My father owns a paint store."

"You come from old pioneer stock then, I suppose."

"I suppose," she said irritably. "Can't we talk about something else . . . like *work?*"

Doug scowled at her. "You're a touchy one, aren't you?"

"A little," Cassie admitted.

"What's the matter? Got a skeleton in the family closet?"

"Not at all," she said. "It's just that I think my typically happy midwestern childhood is a bit dull."

"Why don't you let me be the judge of that?"

"But I have to please myself as well. If I don't enjoy talking about it why should I have to?"

"Because I want to get to know you," Doug said as he took her hand. "I suppose there are other ways for a woman to get to know a man besides talking. Would you like to think of a different way for us to get better acquainted?"

Cassie sat there tensely. Her hand itched to slap him. He was her boss on this job and his behavior was nothing short of sexual harassment. How dare he! But it would be very foolish to alienate Doug. They had too much work ahead of them and they had to be able to get along. She decided to put him off as gently as she could, though she felt a twinge of doubt about her courage. No, she told herself, a true statement was a true statement.

"Doug, I'm not really interested in getting to know *any* man right now."

He gave her a funny look. "You've got to get to know some of us, sweetheart," he said sarcastically. "After all, half the human race is male."

Taking a deep breath, Cassie sat back in her chair. This was going to be tricky. Doug was obviously one of those men with a very fragile ego, the kind of man who makes an overture to a woman and then tries to pretend that he never meant to make an advance as soon as the lady demurs. Cassie had known men like that before. She hated the cat and mouse games that came with that kind of acquaintance.

She looked at him earnestly. "I distinctly remember your saying that you wanted to get to know me as a man gets to know a woman."

"Well, that wasn't what I meant," Doug said.

"Then I guess I misunderstood," Cassie said.

"It's the champagne," he said. "Every time I give a woman champagne she starts thinking about sex." With that, he picked up the bottle and started to pour Cassie another glass.

Quickly, she put her hand over the top of the goblet. "I really shouldn't drink any more."

Doug glared at her. "Can't let this go to waste."

"You said you wanted to shoot this afternoon. The glass I already had relaxed me. But if I drink any more I'm going to start taking pictures of pink elephants instead of real ones."

"Okay, suit yourself," he said as he poured some for himself.

"Are you sure you want to work later on?"

"Absolutely," Doug insisted.

"Then maybe I'll just take a hunk of cheese and some

bread over to the other corner so that I can think about what I'm going to do."

"Sure, if you want to," he agreed tersely. "I have to go over some papers with Jill now anyway."

"Fine," Cassie said. "You know where I'll be if you need me."

"I won't need you," he said, a bit too pointedly.

Cassie took some food and went off by herself. As she fixed a cheese sandwich, she watched Doug take his bottle of champagne over to the rest of the group. Everyone seemed to be joking and having a good time while she felt a little lonely, but at least she'd escaped from Doug.

Monica had managed to wind up sitting near Jack. She was giggling and holding up a sandwich in front of his face. Jack reached up to take the sandwich but Monica slapped playfully at his hand and giggled some more. While she was laughing, Jack quickly snatched the sandwich. Monica stared foolishly at her empty hand. Cassie too was a little wide-eyed at the speed with which Jack had moved. It reminded her of the girl she had known at school who could catch flies barehanded. Jack held up the sandwich and politely gave it back to Monica. This bit of by-play was intensely disturbing to Cassie and she forced herself to turn away from the group.

But she didn't have much luck planning the afternoon's schedule. Her thoughts kept flying between Jack and Doug. It was going to be awkward if Doug tried to continue his pursuit. Most women thought her boss was a dynamic, good-looking man. She agreed that he was conventionally handsome, however she didn't find him dynamic but thought him a very selfish, willful person. And after her experiences with her ex-husband, Cassie wanted to avoid that type of man. What she wanted was someone who was kind, compassionate, and honorable.

Cassie certainly didn't consider Doug's advances very

honorable. Not only was he her employer, but he was still a married man. He claimed to be separated, but still she didn't think it was right for him to approach other women. Cassie stopped herself. Surely, it wasn't *right* for her to impose morals on Doug. Just because she didn't like to be approached by a married man, didn't mean that some other woman wouldn't welcome the attention. All Cassie could be sure of was what she wanted for herself. She knew she didn't want to be involved with a married man ever—or any other man until she was over the past with Larry and well-established on her chosen road into the future.

Before Cassie really had a chance to concentrate on the afternoon's setups, Doug came over to her.

"Let's get out there," he said.

She nodded and quickly finished the rest of her sandwich, then slung her two cameras around her neck and went out onto the observation deck. She looked around her and didn't see any wildlife.

"There are no animals," she said to Doug, who'd been joined by Jack.

"Thanks to you, of course," Doug said irritably.

"I think it's better when we have some wildlife in the shots," she said.

"Don't worry about it. It's okay like this." Doug deliberately turned away from her and went back to his conversation with Jack.

With a shrug Cassie left them. She looked around her. The setting was nice, but there was nothing terribly unusual about it. She would just have to do the best she could. She found Max and the two of them decided on one of the setups that they'd planned to use if there were no animals. The background would be four or five of the sculptures from inside the lounge. Max hurried to arrange everything. Cassie didn't think it looked quite right. They rearranged the sculptures and it still didn't really work. They wanted to work on the background more, but Doug was impatient to get going so they plunged ahead.

When the models came out Cassie didn't quite know what to say. Both of the girls were in baggy striped dresses that made them look like pincushions. She shot an annoyed glance at Doug, who'd never mentioned anything like this particular wardrobe. Cassie just hoped that these outfits weren't among the clothes that were definitely slated to go in the magazine. They were atrocious.

But she started to work although she was still tired from the morning shoot and though nothing in the background or fashions was at all inspiring. She tried to concentrate and make something of the awful setup, but every frame looked forced and unnatural. She started criticizing her work harshly, telling herself that what she was shooting didn't look like live models. She was shooting an ugly still life—pincushions and sculpture. Then even the sculpture became boring and the shots started reminding her of pincushions and clothespins.

She stopped and put her hand over her eyes. The stuff she was doing was terrible. She hated how it looked but she didn't dare breathe a word of criticism aloud. She glanced over at Doug. He was puffing anxiously on a cigar, glaring at her. Beside him stood Jack, arms folded across his chest. A few shaggy dark curls spilled over his forehead and beneath the curls Cassie saw his heavy brows rise and his cold blue eyes bore into her. Both men were watching her so intensely that an enormous wave of self-consciousness rolled over her.

Trying to regain control of herself, she turned back to the models. The striped pincushion dresses looked more ludicrous than ever. Left to her own discretion, Cassie never would have continued. In fact, she probably wouldn't have worked at all that afternoon. However, with Doug standing right there, practically breathing down her neck, she felt she had to keep on trying to do her best, even though the models and the sculpture now began to look to her like bowling pins waiting to be knocked over.

Straightening up, Cassie ran her fingers through her honey gold hair. She'd had it with trying to get this series of shots. It wasn't going to pan out. That was all there was to it. She couldn't stand here for the rest of the afternoon pretending to work. She didn't care if Doug had one of his infamous tantrums. She was finished for the day.

"That's it," Cassie said.

"Pardon me?" Doug said.

Cassie spun around so that she was looking him in the eye. "I said that's all for today."

"I think you can do some more with this setup," he said petulantly.

"No, I can't." She turned and went back into the lounge, fixed herself a cup of coffee, and curled up in one of the comfortable armchairs.

For a moment, she half expected Doug to come roaring into the lounge, screaming at her to get out and finish the session. However, he didn't, and the first person to come through the door was Max, carrying two of the sculptures that they had used for the backdrop.

"Then it's a wrap?" she asked hopefully.

"You called it," Max said with a shrug as he went to bring in the rest of the set.

Then Jack sauntered in, went to the bar, and poured himself a beer. After taking a drink, he turned to stare at Cassie. She stared back but he didn't lower his eyes or look away.

"Well?" she finally said.

He grinned slowly. "I guess you're a bit impertinent, aren't you?"

"Terrific," she replied wryly. "When someone like

you or Doug insists on getting your own way, he's considered authoritative. But let a woman try to have her way and suddenly she's impertinent."

Jack's grin widened. "At least I didn't call you a spitfire. Every time I hear that word I think of some poor serving wench whose shirtsleeves are always being ripped to shreds by a predatory male."

Cassie stared into his cold blue eyes, thinking that right now Jack himself looked the very picture of the "predatory male." "It's comforting to know that you can come up with such a charming mental image," Cassie said with asperity.

"That's a gross misinterpretation," he replied, and then stalked away, so Cassie sat down by herself. The others came into the lounge but she didn't make any effort to communicate with anyone. Doug glanced at her a couple of times, but he didn't approach her.

As soon as the group was ready to leave, she hurried down to maneuver her way to a seat at the very back of the little bus. The two servants got in beside her. They nodded politely and called her "Memsahib." Then they talked quietly between themselves for the rest of the trip. Cassie was able to tune out most of the conversation around her, even Doug's grumbling and Jack's wisecracks. She stared out the window, looking for animals. She did see a mother and baby giraffe back among the trees, but she didn't point them out to the others.

When Jack pulled up, back at the main building of Hillside Resort, Cassie quickly escaped to her room. Once inside, door locked, she sighed heavily. It wasn't that she was expecting anyone. She just wanted to insure her privacy. She threw herself down on the bed, furious that the last series of shots had gone so badly.

She decided that she wasn't even doing to run test prints of that series, although she feared Doug might ask to see them. He might even take a fancy to one of those dreadful shots and decide to put it in the magazine. That just couldn't be allowed and the only way to prevent it was to destroy the film. She took it out of her camera and exposed it to the light, then put the exposed negatives into an ashtray and set fire to them.

As she watched the film burn, Cassie couldn't help feeling that it was a perverse thing to do. But then Doug had been perverse, too, when he'd insisted on her doing extra work. After all, she'd managed to do a very good day's work in a morning. To pressure her into trying for another series was totally unfair—as unfair as it had been to approach her sexually like that!

A knock at the door startled her. "Who is it?" she asked nervously.

"Me!"

It was Monica's voice so Cassie got up to open the door.

"Hiya," said Monica as she walked into the room. "What are you up to?"

"Just thinking," Cassie said.

"Phew! Something stinks!" Monica said, wrinkling up her nose. Then she blushed. "Oops! Hope I didn't offend you."

"How would you offend me?"

"Uh, well, I hope that smell isn't a new perfume. It's pretty awful and everything. But different people have different tastes," Monica said.

"No, it's not a perfume. I was burning something in the ashtray."

"Thank goodness," Monica said. "Looks like I came just in the nick of time."

"What do you mean?"

"Well, Kate and I are going to put hot oil treatments on our hair tonight. We're getting together in my room and we're going to have room service send over dinner. I might even redo my nails. What do you think?"

Cassie was a bit puzzled. She couldn't tell if she was getting an invitation or information. "I think it sounds like a great evening."

"Terrific," Monica said. "Then you'll join us! I don't blame you. I'd do anything to get away from this smell."

Cassie hesitated a moment. She really hadn't meant to accept the invitation. She wasn't at all sure that she wanted any company other than her own. However, when she quickly thought it over, it didn't make much sense to stay in her room alone and mope and dwell on the disturbing events of the day. "Yeah, I think it will be fun. Want me to bring anything?"

Monica shook her head. "Nope. I've got armloads of hair conditioners and facial masks and stuff. You might bring something really awful to wear so you don't get goop all over your good clothes."

"Good idea," Cassie said. She found an old T-shirt that she wore for jogging and tucked it under her arm. Then she followed Monica over to her room.

Kate was already there. Her hair was dripping with oil and she was trying to fit a plastic bag over her scalp.

"This stuff just better work, Monica," Kate said. "If my hair comes out looking like frayed burlap, I'm holding you personally responsible."

"Not to worry," Monica said. "The stuff's great. I mean, I'm addicted to it."

Monica poured some of the hot oil over her own hair and over Cassie's. Then they covered the tops of their heads with plastic and sat down opposite Kate.

Kate started to giggle. "Oh Lordy, I must look as dreadful as you two. I'm just glad the girls at Miss Chesterton's can't see me now."

"I'm just glad that cute little Jonathan What's-a-ma-whoosit can't see me now. He'd be standing there with the body of the century and I'd be sitting here with my head all wrapped in plastic," Monica moaned.

Cassie laughed. "I know what you mean. My hair feels like a gooey peanut butter and jelly sandwich stuffed into a plastic bag."

Monica suddenly had a pouty expression. "Kate's engaged," she announced to Cassie. "Isn't that disgusting? I'm so jealous I could spit."

"Kate! That's wonderful!" Cassie said.

"Randall proposed by mail," Kate said. "It wasn't very romantic, but it did the trick."

"He's loaded, too," Monica said. "Isn't that the pits? Here Kate's got a guy. And Cassie you've had your chance. When am I going to get my turn?"

"I thought you had your eye on Jack?" Kate said.

"Having your eye on a guy and hooking him are two different things," Monica said sadly. "Cassie, how'd you and Larry get together? I mean, I know how Kate met Randall. They belong to the same yacht club and all that. But how'd you meet a rich, handsome man?"

Cassie winced. "Things certainly didn't turn out with Larry the way I'd hoped. And his looks and money were obstacles, not aids to our relationship."

"But at least you got *married*," Monica said. "How old are you anyway?"

"Twenty-seven," Cassie said. "Why?"

"That's just what I mean," Monica said. "You're twenty-seven and already working on number two. I'm twenty-nine and I haven't even scored once."

Cassie's eyes widened as she looked at Monica's childlike face and her baby pink complexion. "You're twenty-nine?"

Nodding, Monica made a face. "Isn't that ghastly? I don't have much time left before the big three-o so I need all the help I can get. The least you can do is take pity on a poor girl and tell her how to snare a cute hunk like your ex."

"Monica, surely you've been asked?" Kate said.

Monica rolled her eyes heavenward. "They were all either too short or too poor. Anyway, Cassie, tell us about Larry."

Sighing, Cassie studied Monica's face. She decided that it wouldn't hurt to tell about her ex-husband. It might even make Monica more cautious about racing headlong into an affair with Jonathan Barton-Hyde. "I don't really know where to begin."

"How'd you meet him?" Monica pressed.

"Out on Long Island," Cassie said, "In the Hamptons. I was going to college in New York and one of my classmates invited me to stay with her family for a weekend."

"Sounds like fun," Kate said.

"Maybe for you," Cassie replied with a little laugh. "After all you grew up with all those polished Easterners. But for a young woman fresh in from Ohio it was all very intimidating."

"But how'd you meet Larry?" Monica pressed.

"Well, my girlfriend, Pamela, noticed that I was feeling lonely and out of place so she organized a game of beach volleyball. It was very thoughtful of her because she knew how much I love team sports. It was the perfect thing to make me relax. Anyway, Larry just happened to be the captain of one of the teams."

"Oo, neat," Monica said.

"That's what I thought at the time," Cassie agreed. "I took one look at those twinkly blue eyes of his and I was hooked."

"I noticed that right away when I first met you two in New York," Monica said. "His blue eyes and your champagne colored mink."

"The mink's gone," Cassie said. "I gave that back when I got disillusioned."

"Oh now, don't go into the depressing part yet," said Kate. "At least not until you've covered the good things."

Cassie laughed. "Okay, okay, so Larry just happened to pick me for his volleyball team. I was really excited and I played as well as I could. I guess I was showing off for him a little."

"You mean your hormones started thumping away right at the very beginning?" Monica squealed.

"Probably. I really liked him. It was instant schoolgirl crush. But I didn't know what to do. He was at least fifteen years older than I was. Plus I was wearing a pair of cutoff jeans and a little boy's T-shirt that I'd bought at a bargain basement sale. I must have looked about twelve in that outfit."

"Gee, I'd give anything to look twelve again," said Monica.

"Monica," Kate said, "let Cassie finish her story."

"Anyway," Cassie continued, "there was supposed to be a big beach cookout that night. I asked Pamela if Larry was going to be there. She said he was, but then she started giving me a lecture about Larry being a quote—menace—unquote."

"She was just jealous," Monica said knowingly.

"Actually, she was telling the truth," Cassie said. "Larry was a bit of a menace. I should have listened to her warning. Instead, I borrowed a sophisticated black cashmere sweater from her and put on my tightest jeans. I went down to the clambake and while I was trying to think of casual ways to approach Larry he came up to me."

"What'd you do? What'd you do?" asked Monica.

"I didn't do anything," Cassie replied. "I just stood there feeling gawky while he went through a routine about how he barely recognized me. Apparently he thought I was a tomboy teenager when he'd met me at the volleyball game."

"So you'd been right," said Kate.

"But that turned out to be a real problem," Cassie

went on. "I thought that I had Larry all figured out since I'd been able to guess exactly what he'd thought of me at that volleyball game. I thought I had everything under control. So I ignored a lot of danger signals."

"How did you mess it up?" Monica asked.

For a moment, Cassie just looked at her. It seemed so strange to look at it that way. All this time, she'd felt that Larry was the one who had ruined things. However, maybe there was something more she could have done than she'd tried.

"Well?" Monica urged.

"He started fooling around—a lot. We had a townhouse in Manhattan. He kept insisting on leaving me there while he went out to the beach house. He tried to pretend that he was alone, but I knew he had girls out there. There wasn't anybody special. It was pretty much a different girl each time."

"Cassie, you should have just ignored it," said Monica.

"I couldn't," Cassie said simply. "I suppose I tried to at first, but then his flirtations became so blatant..." Her voice trailed off. The memories were more painful than she had thought they'd be.

"Blatant?" Monica's brow wrinkled with confusion.

"It was just so obvious that I couldn't pretend I didn't notice."

"Sure you could have," said Monica. "As long as he wasn't planning to leave you."

"I didn't want to live like that," Cassie said.

"But many guys mess around," Monica insisted. "It's normal in some of them and their women just have to learn to live with it."

Cassie studied Monica thoughtfully. With that view it wasn't any wonder that the model was so drawn to Jack and didn't resent his playboy attitude. Cassie glanced over at Kate, who looked troubled. She didn't seem to share Monica's nonchalant attitude about morals.

"I don't know," Cassie said slowly. "I don't know."

Kate looked up and cleared her throat timidly. "Do you mind if we talk about something else?"

"Fine," Cassie said quickly.

"This conversation's getting kind of depressing for somebody's who's just newly engaged," Kate said apologetically.

Chapter Five

CASSIE STARED OUT the window as the minibus bumped along a gravel road. They had left the Hillside Resort early this morning and were now heading into one of the game parks. She had managed to maneuver her way to a window seat, away from both Doug and Jack, and sat quietly, keeping her eyes open for interesting shots.

As she'd expected, Monica had commandeered the place next to Jack. The two of them were keeping up a lively exchange of chatter with Monica giggling appreciatively at every third word he said.

Barry, Kate, Max, and Jill were talking idly. Doug had his pocket calculator out. He was going over columns of figures and frowning. Cassie didn't see him look out the window once.

The bus crossed over a small rise and headed down a long gentle hill. All over the plain ahead of them were hundreds of zebras.

"Holy smokes," Cassie muttered.

Monica squealed. "Zebras! Herds of them!"

"Actually one rather large herd to be precise," said Jack. "If you look carefully you may see a few wildebeests. They've been known to group together."

Cassie strained to see some unusual shape among the herd but each creature she looked at sported a set of perfect black and white stripes. As the bus slowly passed them, Cassie saw some of the closer animals raise their heads and peer solemnly into the bus's interior. But while she and the rest strained to get a good look at the zebras, the animals, in contrast, seemed only mildly curious about them.

"They seem bored with us," Cassie said to no one in particular.

"They are," Jack replied with a mischievous wink. "After you've been out in the bush for a week you'll have seen so many zebras that you'll begin to understand how they feel about us. But for now you can enjoy the novelty."

Cassie just glared at Jack. He seemed to be making a point of flaunting his superior knowledge of Africa, his tone constantly mocking in response to every word she said.

As the bus slowly left the zebras behind, Cassie started looking diligently for more animals. She didn't see anything for a while, but then she spotted some dark shapes off in the distance. She couldn't quite tell what sort of animals they were and she didn't want to start up a conversation with Jack again, so she remained silent and watched the shapes disappear behind the next rise. A little further on they saw about ten zebras. Already Cassie could see what Jack meant. The group in the bus looked at these zebras far less eagerly than they had looked at the first herd.

When they reached the game park lodge, Doug had what he considered to be a brilliant idea. He wanted Cassie to do a series of shots of Monica and Kate in black and white sports outfits with the herd of zebras. Although Cassie feared that the shots might look a little too hokey, she also felt that they might be able to have some fun with that particular setup. She agreed to do it.

While Monica and Kate went off to change, Cassie and Doug looked for Jack, who had strolled away. They found him with two Kikuyu men, conversing in Swahili. Cassie hesitated a moment, waiting for Jack to finish with the men. Doug glared at the Kikuyus irritably. Then he just interrupted them.

"Uh . . . Jack, we've got to set up a shot. Right away," he said.

Cassie's face was hot with embarrassment. The Kikuyus seemed to handle the situation gracefully, but she couldn't help feeling humiliated to be with Doug, who had treated them so rudely. Jack seemed to smooth the situation over. He said something in Swahili about "the bwana," which made the men laugh. She guessed that he'd made a joke out of Doug's lack of courtesy. Whatever he said seemed to set the Kikuyu men at ease and they walked away with dignity. For a moment, she felt a glimmer of respect for Jack.

Suddenly he turned and caught her eye. Cassie had always been told that she had the kind of expressive face that gave away what she was thinking. She looked down quickly so that he wouldn't see the gleam of admiration in her eyes. She didn't want him to think that he had any sort of upper hand with her at all. She might be impressed with the way he dealt with his countrymen, but she did not approve of the way he treated women. She wanted to make that clear to him at all costs.

"Ms. Dearborn," Jack said urbanely. "I can't tell you how flattered I am that you're so pleased with me."

Cassie kept her eyes pinned to the ground. Obviously her expression *had* given her away. She'd have to be extremely cautious around Jack from now on. Otherwise, she'd just encourage him to needle her even more.

Fortunately, Doug was so eager to get to work that he jumped in and took Jack's attention away from Cassie. "I've got a great idea," he said. "We've got to get rolling so we can be set up by the time the light is right."

"Fine," Jack said. "What do you need?"

"I want to take a couple of shots of the girls in the middle of the herd."

Jack's jaw dropped and he just stared at Doug. Finally he spoke. "It's a joke, isn't it? Some sort of American humor?"

"You got a problem with American humor?" Doug asked belligerently. But at Jack's level, hard-eyed gaze he visibly retreated, adding quickly, "If you have a problem with this shoot, then I'll do the setup myself."

"You know perfectly well that it's strictly forbidden for you to go into any parks or game reserves on your own," Jack said. "You're required to have an authorized guide."

"I can manage on my own," Doug insisted.

"Obviously, you can't," Jack said with a superior air. Cassie could feel her animosity toward him rising again. "If you knew what you were doing," he went on, "you wouldn't suggest such a ridiculous scheme. Now I'll grant you that the zebra may not be the most thrilling creature in the world but it is still a wild animal. Your models could easily be kicked, bitten, or trampled. It may not trouble your conscience much if one of those girls got hurt but it would certainly trouble mine."

"I'm going to shoot them with the zebras and that's final," Doug said. He was trying to stay controlled but Cassie could tell that he was really furious. She glanced anxiously at Jack.

He looked thoughtful, unimpressed by Doug's emotion, but turned to Cassie. "There is one way to do it," he said. "The only way."

Now Doug seemed to calm down a little bit as well. "What's that?"

"The models and the photographer have to stay inside the vehicles," Jack said firmly.

Doug waved his hands angrily. "No, no, can't do it. I don't want pictures of them waving through a car window. That doesn't sell magazines!"

"They could stand up in the sunroof opening," Jack

suggested. "That's how most tourists see Africa anyway."

Instantly, Cassie brightened. She liked that idea very much. It would be a far more natural looking setup than the one that Doug had suggested. Also, she felt that Jack did have a point about the animals being dangerous.

"I like it, Doug," she said quickly. "I think it will be better."

Almost before she'd finished speaking, Doug and Jack had both turned to stare at her. Cassie realized that she'd thrown herself into the middle of their argument. It was too late to back off now. She stood looking from one to the other.

"What did you say?" Doug asked.

"I think it might be a better setup," Cassie said. "It would be more realistic, less..." she broke off, trying to think of a polite word for "hokey." "...less stylized," she said finally.

"Okay, we'll try it," Doug surprised her by saying.

Cassie was relieved. The fight was over and she was going to get a better series of shots. Then she noticed that Doug was looking at her strangely. She realized that he'd changed the setup as a concession to her. Nervously she wondered if he'd expect her to do him a "favor" in return.

Jack arranged for one of the Kikuyu men to drive Doug, Barry, and the models over to the zebra herd. Cassie and Jack followed in a jeep. She didn't really want to ride alone with him, yet there was no alternative as the other vehicle was filled.

Leaning her head back against the seat, she looked across at him. The wind was blowing Jack's dark curls off his face. In profile, his strong chin and high cheekbones made him look like one of those terribly handsome heroes of the silent movie era. Cassie smiled at the notion that he might see himself in heroic terms.

Just then he glanced at her sharply. "What is it?"

"I was just thinking that you've probably decided that you're going to rescue me from any vicious zebra attacks," said Cassie with mock concern in her voice.

"I wouldn't be so cocky if I were you, Ms. Dearborn." He smiled wickedly. "After all, I already have rescued you from a baboon, haven't I?"

Suddenly Cassie noticed a bush ahead that was shaking violently. At first she thought this might be caused by the wind, but then glancing around she noticed that the other trees and bushes were swaying with a far different, more gentle rhythm. She strained to get a better look at the quivering bush, but as she watched it stopped shaking. Then the erratic motions started up again more wildly than ever.

"What in hell is that?" she said softly.

"Pardon?" Jack asked.

"That bush over there," Cassie said as she pointed to the little tree which was now quaking with a frenzy.

"Good Lord," Jack muttered. "If I were a superstitious person, I'd think we were having ghostly visitations."

"Then that's not normal?" Cassie asked nervously.

"Hardly," he replied. "Let's go take a look. Shall we?"

Cassie nodded, though she could feel her throat tightening with fear, and Jack started driving toward the bush. She was glad that he was proceeding slowly and cautiously. Ironically now she was pleased that he was there to protect her. Out of the corner of her eye she saw him take a gun out of his holster and hold it in readiness.

"Don't worry," he said, "it's only a tranquilizer gun and I probably won't have to use it."

Cassie nodded.

"Do you see anything?" he asked.

"Nothing."

He cautiously edged the jeep forward about ten feet and then stopped again.

"Just what are we looking for?"

"I'm not sure." He inched the jeep forward, stared at the tree, and then smiled gently.

The bush started moving again as Jack said, "It's a little Thomson's gazelle."

"A Thomson's gazelle? I wouldn't know what one of those was if it ate me alive for breakfast."

"That would be highly unlikely," said Jack. Then he added, "Stay here."

Taking his gun, he started to get out of the jeep.

"I thought you said those gazelle things were harmless," Cassie said.

"They are," Jack said. "However, you never know what else may be lurking about."

Cassie strained to look into the bushes, and finally saw the animal. It was the most delicate little antelope, about the size of a collie, but far more slimly built. Its coat was a light dun color with a stripe of black and a stripe of white on each side, and its head sported two short-pronged antlers. The gazelle stood stock still except for its tiny tail, which flicked anxiously as Jack approached.

Suddenly Jack stopped. "Damn," he exclaimed.

"What is it?" Cassie asked.

He turned to look at her. "If this is a poacher's trap, somebody's going to pay."

The anger and violence that accompanied his threat startled, then deeply pleased Cassie. She felt even more pleasure hearing his voice croon to the little gazelle. "Take it easy, little Thommy. Don't you worry about old Jack here. The last thing he wants to do is hurt you."

He walked steadily toward the frightened little creature. For a moment it looked ludicrous to see a grown man chatting with a deer, but quickly she realized there was a kindness in Jack that seemed to bridge the gulf between man and animal. The gazelle almost seemed to be listening to what he was saying.

Then suddenly Jack took another step closer and the spell was broken. The animal began to thrash around violently, desperately trying to get away and, Jack moved fast to close the gap between himself and the gazelle. The frightened animal tried to butt at him with its tiny antlers. Jack grabbed an antler in one hand and scooped his other hand under the animal's belly.

Quickly, Cassie grabbed her camera and photographed the scene as it unfolded in front of her. Jack held the animal in a vice-tight grip and it stopped struggling.

"Take it easy, little Thommy," he said. "Your heart doesn't need to pound so hard. I'm hardly about to eat you."

Cassie saw the little gazelle roll his eyes until he was looking into Jack's face. The total helplessness of the creature touched her so much that she almost got out of the jeep and went to help. Then she remembered Jack's order and stayed where she was.

"Now let's see what the problem is," he said as he shifted the creature's weight around. "Ah! We've gotten ourselves stuck pretty nastily, haven't we?" The gazelle struggled a little and Jack tightened his grip. "Now how am I going to get you out of here if you don't settle down?" As if he'd understood, the gazelle was quiet again. Jack was able to run a practiced hand over the animal's spindly leg. "Doesn't look as if you've broken anything. Let's see if we can't get you out of this mess."

With a few deft movements, Jack managed to free the Thomson's gazelle. Then he released the animal and stepped back a few paces. For a moment, the deer just lay there quietly. Then it stood up and took a few hesitant steps. Cassie could see that one of its back legs didn't look quite right.

"He's limping!" she said.

"Naturally his leg's a bit stiff," said Jack, keeping his

eyes on the gazelle. "However, nothing's broken. He should be all right as long as he gets back to his herd fairly soon."

"Was it a poacher's trap?"

"Fortunately not."

The gazelle took a tentative bound forward, then another wobbly leap and another. Finally the little creature seemed steadier on his feet and he scampered away.

"That appears to be that," said Jack, and turned back to Cassie. She felt a tremendous warmth coming from the man. Also, the kindness that he had shown to the little gazelle had touched her. She softened.

Their eyes locked. Cassie slowly got out of the jeep and stood with her back to the fender as Jack moved toward her. There was a dreamlike quality to the moment and her heart began to thunder as her breath came in fast, shallow gulps. Something electric, infinitely exciting was passing between them and her intellect had no part to play in it... only her feelings. And then a rocket went off within her, sending wildfire along every nerve ending.

Jack's arms whipped her hard against his body. One hand rose to cradle the base of her skull, then tilt her head back. His lips were hot on hers as he kissed her hungrily, his head moving side to side slowly but with such force that her lips felt flayed, maddeningly so. She savored the experience. Her lips were tingling in a way that was oddly new and set off a flurry of sensations that made her loins ache.

The direction of the movement of Jack's head changed to a slow nod and with each upward stroke his tongue flicked at her swollen mouth. Slowly, ever so slowly... with a hypnotizing passion... he brought her lips apart. Her mouth open wide between quivering lips, eyes closed, head thrown back, Cassie awaited him in thrall.

Jack had pulled away slightly and now with a groan he lowered his head again, his tongue thrusting full into the soft sweetness of her waiting mouth. Probing, darting, lightly flicking, their tongues explored . : . challenged. Cassie was wildly abandoned to the moment. It registered somewhere in the back of her mind that this was sheer insanity, but her feelings commanded, not her logical brain. Instinct drove her to accept every sensation as completely right, totally perfect.

In a frenzy her hands moved on his chest, palms tingling as they ran over the hair at the V in his shirt. She pressed her body close against the whole long, hard length of him. Her hands moved around his neck and her fingers burrowed into the thick richness of the hair that grew long to his collar.

His lips were as greedy as her hands, which moved down the strong column of his neck, over his broad shoulders. His hot mouth traveled moistly over her throat and drew soft little moans of pleasure from her. He nipped at her ear, ran his tongue along its spiralled pinkness, trailed fiery kisses along her jaw. His lips found hers again. His hands were on her buttocks and as their kiss deepened, they ground their hips against each other's.

Cassie heard Jack's long, anguished whistle of breath before he pulled away from her.

Spellbound, she returned his penetrating stare. Both of them were breathing in tortured gasps and their bodies trembled as the little gazelle's had.

Jack found his voice first. "So it *is* mutual," he said huskily, a half-smile curving the corners of his mouth. "At last you've admitted you want me as much as I want you."

Cassie badly needed the support of the jeep. She turned, elbows resting on the fender, her head in her hands. Lord, what had possessed her to succumb to this

man in this moment? She didn't love him—she didn't
even like him! It was just that tenderness he'd shown the
tiny animal, she told herself. It had hit at a great, gaping
wound inside her and made her want that same gentling
and salvation for herself. Divorcee, she spat silently at
herself, hungry for love.

"Come on, Cassie," he said coaxingly, bent close to
her ear. "You *have* admitted it."

"Glands can't talk!" she hurled over her shoulder.

"Glands? Glands!" He repeated the word first in question, then outrage. "So you think that's all there was to
this, eh?"

She whirled to face him and pushed him back with
the flat of her hands. "What else could there be, Jack?
Unless in some weird way you were punishing me. We
aren't even friends, you know."

He let out a sound of total disgust. "You're impossible, woman." He strode around to the driver's side of
the jeep and nodded curtly for her to resume her seat.
"Pull yourself together," he commanded. "It wouldn't
have gone further than it did out here. I like my women
in nice soft beds in rooms with locks, not out in the wild
where I can't really concentrate on my lovemaking."

"Your *women!* Your *lovemaking!* You're as con-
temptible a womanizer as I've ever run into. . . . As I
suspected you were. Well you can keep your hands off
me from this moment until the twelfth of never, Mr.
Barton-Hyde."

"The twelfth of never? Hmm-m, we'll just have to
see about that, Ms. Dearborn."

By the time they arrived at the herd of zebras, Doug
was as furious with her as she was with Jack. He leaned
out the bus window and screamed. "Where the hell have
you two been?"

"Couldn't be helped," Jack said calmly\

Doug glared at them. "This isn't Lovers' Lane out here you know."

Cassie went hot and glanced at Jack. He was looking at her, smiling that odd grin which had made her uncomfortable in the past and now enraged her. "I can assure you, Douglas," he said with mock solemnity, "Lovers' Lane may have been Ms. Dearborn's destination, but it was hardly mine."

Cassie glared at Jack. She could feel the white heat of anger suffusing her and she longed to shriek at him. However, she knew she'd never get herself under control for the afternoon's photo session if she didn't put a quick end to this scene.

She looked back at Doug. He was staring at her possessively. It was obvious that Jack's remark had made him jealous. Monica was sitting next to Doug and she didn't look very pleased either. The whole situation was just so ridiculously awkward!

"Look, Doug," she said irritably. "Next time you want to do one of these two car shoots don't put me with this idiot, please. You know how he gets on my nerves."

Cassie didn't even bother to look for Jack's reaction. She just noticed that Doug seemed placated and Monica brightened considerably.

"Yeah," said Monica. "Let Jack drive *us*. That'll be fun."

"Let's just get to work," Doug said curtly.

"Roger. Over and out," Monica said.

Cassie picked up her camera and clicked off a couple of candid shots of Monica getting herself settled on the rim of the sunroof.

"Hey, what do you think, Cassie?" Monica yelled. "Do I look like a zebra or what?"

Cassie just laughed and waved back.

"She looks rather more like a gazelle," Jack said

softly. "I should think our friend Doug missed his perfect shot."

Pretending not to have heard him, Cassie went right on with her work. However, she couldn't stop herself from thinking that Monica *did* have the same spindly grace as the little gazelle that Jack had rescued. Remembering the expression on Jack's face when he'd saved the animal, Cassie shivered. She sternly forced down the images that came to mind about what followed.

She thanked heaven for the concentration her work demanded and started clicking off shots of Monica. Then she worked with Kate and Monica together before taking Kate solo.

She was especially pleased with a series of zany-looking pictures of the two models staring two zebras in the eye. That seemed to capture the thought she'd had earlier that the tourists amused the animals as much as the animals amused the tourists. She was still going strong when Jack called a halt to everything.

Scowling, Cassie looked over at him. "I want to stay a little longer. Just a half hour."

"As much as I'd like to oblige you, my dear Ms. Dearborn," he said, "I'm afraid that you'll have to stop."

"Why? Because you say so?" she asked.

"Precisely."

"I get it. The great white hunter speaks and all must obey. Charming."

"This isn't a power struggle, Ms. Dearborn," he said as he slowly inspected her figure. Cassie had the humiliating feeling that she'd opened her shirt one button too far. She fought the urge to quickly close the collar of her blouse and instead she stared back at him angrily. Her attitude didn't seem to intimidate Jack at all. It only amused him. "However, if you're looking for a power struggle or any other struggle for that matter," he said,

"I'd be only too willing to oblige."

"I'd like to be left alone. And I'd like to get my work done," Cassie said. "So if you'll stop playing games, I'll get back to what I was doing. *I'll* let you know when I'm ready to go."

"And I suppose the great novice photographer would like to turn her charming little backside into lion meat?"

"What are you going to do? Strand me out here?" she asked. "I thought you Englishmen were supposed to be so polite?"

"Since you obviously haven't noticed, let me point out that the sun is setting. It isn't terribly wise to ride around the plains in an open jeep at night. Or hadn't you thought of that?"

Cassie sighed. "You could have said as much in the first place."

"I thought you photographers were supposed to be so observant," said Jack dryly. "However, next time I'll be happy to do you the honor of underestimating your intelligence."

Slumping down on the seat, Cassie didn't say any more. Jack drove the jeep over to the small bus and explained that they had to get back to the lodge by nightfall. He exchanged a few words in Swahili with the Kikuyu driver and they started back.

As Cassie gazed out at the dusky terrain, she felt a wave of exhaustion pass over her. She always felt full of vitality while she was working, but by the end of the day she was totally drained. Today she had more reason to feel drained than ever.

"You look pensive," Jack said. "I suppose you're savoring delicious memories of our tryst out here in Lovers' Lane?"

Cassie didn't want to dignify that snide remark with a reply. She sat still, feeling tears well in her eyes and resolutely blinked them back. Surely she would never have been subjected to these embarrassing remarks if she were another woman. In fact, Monica was proof of that. She was actively pursuing Jack, and although her actions were a little transparent, he was never rude or inconsiderate in public. Cassie's thoughts strayed to how he behaved in *private*.

"You're being a bit antisocial for a socialite," Jack said.

"My ex-husband may have been a socialite, but I never was. Besides, between the two of us, you're the one who's in the strong social position."

"Me?" Jack seemed incredulous.

"Don't you remember your lecture about how you owned a hotel and a game park and a coffee plantation?"

"Yes, I do. I also distinctly remember your telling me all that was worthless."

"Perhaps it's not," she said carefully. Jack didn't seem to be about to make a joke out of her statement so she continued. "I do think that something like your hotel has value as a measure of one's accomplishment. I mean, it must give you a wonderful feeling of security to know that you've created something beautiful."

"Well, I was hardly the architect..." Jack began.

"But you had the taste to choose the architect and the location and so forth," she insisted.

"Yes, I suppose whatever's there has old Jack's stamp on it," he concurred. "What's the point of all this?"

"Well," said Cassie. Then she hesitated. She was afraid to tell Jack her real feelings. She was worried that if she let him see what she was really thinking he might turn around and use that knowledge against her. On the other hand, she *wanted* to tell him. More, she wanted to make an appeal to him.

"You were about to say?" he asked with an eyebrow raised.

"There is a point to this," she said tentatively. "I'm

just trying to figure out where to begin."

"Take your time."

"You see, I'd like to do what you've done. I'd like to create something really lovely that I could be proud of."

"That seems like a reasonable ambition."

"The trouble is," she said nervously, "I feel like you're getting in my way. It's making me crazy."

"Me?"

"I know I brought it on myself," she said quickly. "I kind of jumped down your throat that first day at the hotel and—"

"Yes," he interrupted, chuckling, "you were a *bit* feisty."

"I'm sorry," she said. "Do you want to hear my excuses?"

Jack slowed the jeep and turned to look at her. "If you want to tell me you may. But please don't feel that I'm demanding an explanation. I'll be happy to do you the courtesy of assuming that you had good cause for your actions."

"I don't know whether I did or not. All I know is that I'm having trouble getting into my work here. I can't seem really to unwind at the end of the day. And it's hard to maintain my concentration during the day."

"I see," Jack said, as his lips pulled into a thin line.

"After we got to Hillside, I thought we'd made an arrangement to stay out of each other's way."

"I wouldn't count that little tiff we had in front of our friend Douglas as an arrangement."

"Obviously not," she said. "You've been bothering me and needling me every chance you've had. I really can't handle any more."

"Then you haven't managed to develop that sense of humor as you promised to do."

"I guess not." She cleared her throat. "But then, you

haven't kept out of my way as you promised to do."

Jack was quiet for a moment. Cassie sat anxiously, waiting for him to make some comment. She was uncertain about the whole course of this conversation. Jack was being far more considerate and attentive than she had dared to hope. However, she still had a nagging fear that his kindness was part of some horrible joke or might backfire in some other way.

"I really wish I understood exactly what problems you're fretting about," he said at last.

"Well, this job means an awful lot to me. As you pointed out I am a bit of a novice. I haven't done a whole lot of photography work yet. This is a great break for me. But it's been a real ordeal."

"And I'm the cause of this ordeal?" he asked.

"You're part of the cause," she replied.

Jack nodded.

"It . . . it goes back to what I was saying before about wanting to create something beautiful. I want—no, I *need*—to do really good work. And to have a lot of people see my pictures. But, I'm so afraid that if I ruin my chances with this job I may never get another break."

Jack looked thoughtful for a moment before he spoke. "You said earlier that you believed I had managed to create something worthwile . . . at the resort."

"Yes," Cassie said tentatively, wondering where this was leading.

"Then take it from someone who knows. You can accomplish what you want. You don't need this break. You don't need any favors. Because what you have to offer will be valuable."

She smiled. Half because she was surprised to see Jack being so serious. Half because she thought what he was saying sounded like platitudes. "Seems to me I've heard that before. The American dream. Everybody can get whatever he wants. Everybody can be President.

Trouble is at least two guys run every year and one of them can't be 'lucky'."

"My dear Cassie," Jack said. "I come from a long line of British aristocrats. No one in my family has ever claimed that *everyone* can get whatever he or she wants. Nor did I say that." He paused. "I said that *you* could do whatever you set out to do."

She was so moved she thought she might lose all control and throw herself onto him, weeping. She steadied herself. Then, resolutely she said, "If I'm really able to do anything I set out to do, why can't I persuade you to leave me alone?"

"You *have* persuaded me," Jack said. "Surely I'm not offending you now."

"Not now," Cassie admitted. "But what about the rest of the trip. Will you promise to stay away from me?"

Taking his eyes off the narrow road, Jack stared full at her. "Are you sure that's what you want?"

"Yes," Cassie said firmly.

"Then I promise to keep my distance," Jack said solemnly. "I hope you don't mind if I talk to you in the line of work. It would be damned awkward if we didn't speak at all." After a pause he added, "I'm terribly sorry if I hurt you. I really didn't intend to do that."

Cassie didn't reply. The man astounded her with the contrasts he presented to her.

Chapter Six

CASSIE HURRIED OUT of the darkroom clutching a pile of test prints against her chest. She hadn't gone more than a few steps when she ran right into another person.

"Sorry," she muttered before she even glanced up to see who it was. Then she looked up with an apologetic smile which quickly faded at the sight of Jack. An odd little smile played around the corners of his mouth. Cassie couldn't tell if the smile was meant to be kind or to show some sort of cruel satisfaction. In any case, it agitated her so that she backed away a couple of steps.

"Oh, it's you," she muttered. Cassie hadn't spoken more than a few words to him in the last few days since their serious talk, when she had asked him to let her concentrate on her work. He'd kept his distance and behaved like a perfect gentleman... too perfect she sometimes thought, and waited for the cloudburst. At any moment he might revert to being that argumentative man with the biting tongue—or the lover—and she didn't know which would be worse for her peace of mind.

"I see," said Jack as his smile broadened. "If you'd known that it was me you ran into, you wouldn't have bothered to apologize. Correct?"

"That's not what I said," she replied. The unexpected meeting had caught her off guard. She gripped the pile of test sheets close against her chest, as though it were some sort of protective shield.

"Well, in that case, I'll assume that the apology was freely given and I'll accept it gladly," Jack said in such a gallant tone of voice that Cassie wondered if he might be mocking her somehow.

She looked up at him in a challenging way, but didn't say anything.

"How are you enjoying the trip so far?" he asked.

"Oh, it's fine. It's great." Good Lord, she thought, how witless she sounded. She was uncomfortably aware, too, that she looked awfully shabby. She was wearing her sloppiest darkroom jeans and T-shirt. Her hair was pulled back into a pony tail and she didn't have on one dab of makeup. Nervously, she brushed her hand over a few stray wisps of hair.

"You've become quite an animal expert," Jack said.

"Oh, come on!"

"Well, you've done better than the rest of the people in your group. You can tell the difference between a Thomson's Gazelle, a Grant's Gazelle and an Impala. Everyone else keeps lumping antelopes together as 'those funny looking deer.'"

"It's part of my job," she explained. "I like to know exactly what I'm photographing."

"It's nice to know that you take pride in being so thorough in your work," Jack said.

"Thanks," Cassie said. She was feeling terribly self-conscious. "Listen," she said. "I was looking for Doug. Have you seen him?"

Jack's expression seemed to cloud. "Yes, he's back in the lounge. As I was leaving he was drinking a martini and toying with his pocket calculator."

"I'd better go then," she said quickly. She bolted away before Jack had a chance to say anything more.

They were staying at a game park lodge deep in Tanzania. The lodge had rooms facing onto a central court-yard. Off to the west of the lodge itself was a beautiful garden. On the south side of the courtyard were the lounge, the dining room, and the darkroom. It didn't take long for Cassie to rush along the south edge of the courtyard and into the lounge where Doug was going over some figures with his pocket calculator, as Jack had said. By this time, though, Doug was working on his second martini.

Quietly, she walked over to him. "Doug?"

He looked up at her eagerly. She thought she saw the same glint in his eyes that was there when he asked her to go out for a walk alone or something comparable. Lately, he had been a little more persistent than she would have liked, so she decided to get down to business as quickly as possible before he got the wrong idea. She handed him the manila envelope full of pictures.

"What do you think of these?" she asked.

Anxiously, she watched as Doug pulled the pictures out of the envelope. He leafed through the pile quickly. Then he went through it again. This time he looked much more slowly. He grunted once. Cassie's throat went dry. She didn't know whether it was a sign of approval or disapproval. She began to wonder if he wasn't savoring this moment, and decided to prompt him to make some kind of comment, even if it was negative.

"Well?"

"I'd say you're on the right track. Definitely on the right track," he said as he leaned back in his chair and nodded thoughtfully.

"Really?" Cassie was unable to hold back a grin.

"Yes, these are quite good. But I don't want you getting a swollen head. I'll expect you to do even better on the rest of the assignment."

"I will," said Cassie. "I think the longer I'm out here the more I know how to shoot Africa."

Doug didn't respond to the remark. He merely inclined his head in the direction of the seat next to him. "Why don't you sit down and have a drink?" he said casually. "Then we can go over the photos together."

Cassie felt uncomfortable. The last thing she wanted to do was to sit drinking with Doug while he pretended to go over her pictures, using his comments and criticism as a way of maintaining control or trying to exert power over her.

"I don't know, Doug," she said. "I really should get a few more test prints done and clean up the darkroom."

He frowned. "I need to give you some input on these. That was the whole point of having you run up test prints—to get the editor's criticism."

"I'll tell you what."

"What?" he asked a little too eagerly.

"Why don't you write your comments on the back of each of the photos? That way I can pick them up later and study them very carefully."

"I think we should go over them together," he said.

Cassie gave him the calmest, most patient smile she could manage. "I work better on my own, Doug. I really do. It'll be so much better if I can just go over your comments alone."

"What if you don't understand what they mean?"

"I can always ask you questions later, can't I?"

"Maybe we should..."

The sound of Monica's high, nervous laugh interrupted Doug. Turning around, Cassie saw that the model had tripped or stumbled against the entrance to the lounge.

"Boy, oh boy," Monica giggled as she noticed that Cassie and Doug were looking at her. "I'm about as clumsy as a cross-eyed hippo. I mean, do you believe that I just ran into a door?"

"Are you okay?" asked Cassie.

"Sure," said Monica. "I just wish I were as graceful as those funny looking deer."

"I wouldn't worry about that," Cassie said. "You always manage to look just right, Monica."

It was true. Today, as always, Monica looked smashing. She had on a beautiful lavender raw silk dress, which made her look paler than usual. Cassie felt even more self-conscious about her sloppy darkroom clothes.

"Hey, have you guys seen Jack?" Monica asked. "He said he'd meet me in here."

"I saw him outside a few minutes ago," Cassie said. "He was..."

A form appeared in the doorway to the lounge and Monica suddenly grinned. "Hiya Jack. I was just asking about you." She moved toward him, but stopped suddenly. She was swaying and reached out to grip the back of a chair to steady herself.

Something was very wrong and, alarmed, Cassie headed toward her as Jack and Doug exchanged an uneasy glance.

"What is it?" asked Cassie gently.

Monica shrugged.

"Do you feel dizzy?"

"Umm..." Monica said as a slight look of panic crossed her face.

"Are you tired?"

Monica nodded. Cassie felt the model's forehead. It was hot and damp.

"Maybe you'd better lie down," Cassie said. Then she turned to Doug and Jack. "I'll take Monica back to her room. Maybe one of you guys should try to find a doctor."

"I don't need a doctor," Monica said weakly. "Don't you dare get me one."

"But if you're sick..." said Cassie.

"I'm just tired. Maybe I *should* go back to my room. I'll be okay once I rest."

"You're sure?" Jack asked. Cassie caught a note of

genuine concern in his voice.

"Scout's honor," Monica said as she held up her hand in a little salute. "I'm just tired and I'm feeling kind of punchy."

"I'll walk back with you," Cassie volunteered and steered her out of the room. She steadied Monica as they left the building.

"Gee, I feel dizzy," Monica said, shuffling rather than walking along the path.

"We're almost there," Cassie replied.

Taking Monica's keys from her, she opened the door to the room. Monica hurried inside. She ripped off the lavender silk dress and tossed it over a chair. As Cassie picked up the dress and put it on a hanger, Monica flopped down on the bed.

"How *do* you feel?" Cassie asked. "Really?"

"Well, I sure needed to lie down. I can tell you that much."

"Do you want to get under the covers?"

"Oh, all right," Monica said. "I suppose I should."

Feebly, she managed to crawl into the bedclothes. Cassie tried to help her but was pushed away. Monica lay still for a moment, staring up at the ceiling. Finally, she turned to Cassie and muttered, "Isn't Jack dreamy looking?"

"He's a very handsome man," Cassie said cautiously.

"I just wish he'd get a haircut," Monica said in a small, soft voice. Suddenly, she bolted upright and looked around with wild feverish eyes. "Oh no! I think I'm gonna...I think I'm gonna..." Then she put her head in her hands. "Oh boy."

"What is it?" Cassie asked.

"I just felt kind of sick. I think I'm okay now."

Monica looked terribly weak and pale. Cassie thought she seemed to be quite ill. "I wonder if you might have a fever, Monica. Maybe I'd better check."

Monica glared at her. "Cassie, I swear if you come after me with one of those thermometers I'll bite it in two."

"All right. Forget I mentioned it."

"And I don't want a doctor."

"Can't I do something for you?"

"Let me rest. That's all," Monica said. "You've been a doll and all that, but I just want a nap."

"Okay, I'll leave you alone," Cassie said. Then she took a note pad and wrote her room number on it. "This is my room. If you need anything, call me."

"Right-o." Monica lay back in bed and pulled the covers up over herself.

"Don't you want to put on your nightgown or brush your teeth or anything?"

"Nope. Just a little snooze is all I need."

"Okay," Cassie said as she turned off the lights and slipped out of the room.

As she walked back toward the darkroom, she couldn't help worrying. She was sure that Monica was sicker than she would admit. Cassie wasn't sure what she ought to do about it.

"Ms. Dearborn."

Cassie was so involved with her own thoughts that the voice totally startled her and she jumped half a foot.

"You scared me," she muttered, now face to face with Jack.

"Yes," he said dryly, "I'd noticed."

Cassie didn't reply.

"I realize that you don't want me to approach you," he said. "But in this case it's necessary. It's about Monica."

"Oh."

"I'm worried that she might be quite sick. You felt her forehead. Was she feverish?"

"I thought so," Cassie replied.

"Oh dear," Jack said thoughtfully.

Cassie looked into his eyes and saw the same tenderness now that she'd seen the time he freed the little gazelle. She didn't know quite what to make of it. She never would have thought he was the kind of man who would show compassion for a sick woman he scarcely knew. Yet, compassion was written all over his face. She swallowed hard at the knowledge that Monica had managed to stir up strong feelings in this cynical man.

"Do you think we ought to do something?" she asked.

"I have a thermometer in my first aid kit," Jack said. "Maybe at the least you should dash in before she falls asleep and take her temperature."

"I offered to earlier. She said she wouldn't let me."

"That's absurd."

"I know," Cassie said. "I think she's afraid of doctors. I think that's why she doesn't want to admit that she's sick."

"That's awkward, isn't it?"

She nodded. "I was just trying to figure out how to handle the situation when you startled me."

"Did you come up with any solutions?"

"Not really," she said.

"I hate to see her take chances with her health," Jack said. "She seems like such a fragile woman. It makes me worry."

"Even though she looks fragile, she was always pretty healthy when I knew her in New York. She's not really a sickly person."

A frown appeared between Jack's thick, dark brows. "I hate to interfere in someone else's business," he said, "but the idea of Monica lying there in that room, sick and alone, makes me very uneasy."

Cassie studied his expression. It was obvious that he was genuinely concerned. "I gave Monica my room number and told her to call me if she needed anything."

"You did?" said Jack with a much more cheerful expression.

"Yes and I'm sure she'll call if she feels any worse."

"Of course, she will."

"Besides, it's probably one of those twenty-four hour things. I'll bet she'll be fine after a good night's rest."

"I hope so," Jack replied. Then he didn't say anything. He just stared at Cassie until she felt the need to flee.

"I'd better run," she said. "I've got a lot of work to do yet tonight." She refused to let herself run, but she did walk awfully fast away from him. Up to now Cassie had thought that if there were anything at all developing between Jack and Monica it was only an idle flirtation. But there was a little more to it than that. At least there seemed to be on his part.

Jack was all Monica claimed she wanted in a man— handsome, sexy, wealthy, *tall!* Despite how awful she felt, Cassie had to smile at that last descriptive. She brought her hand to her eyes and rubbed them. Lord, what a fool she was. She'd demanded he stay away from her, thereby giving him a good hard shove in Monica's direction, and now she was miserable because she'd got what she asked for.

The next morning, Cassie decided that she'd better check on Monica first thing. She got dressed quickly in a pair of khaki shorts and a matching man-tailored shirt. She left the shirt unbuttoned at the neck and rolled the sleeves up, which gave the outfit a jaunty, sporty look. Then she combed the tangles out of her hair, put on a little bit of makeup, slipped into a pair of sandals, and hurried off to Monica's room.

She knocked on the door. There was no answer. For a moment, Cassie thought that Monica might already be awake and off to breakfast. Just to double check, she knocked a second time. Then she heard something fall over inside.

"Monica!" she cried. "Are you all right?"

"Just knocked over a lamp," was the feeble reply. Suddenly the door flew open. Monica still had on the slip that she'd fallen asleep in. Her normally thin face looked much too gaunt, and she had dark circles under her eyes which were accentuated by runny mascara.

"How are you feeling?" Cassie asked gently.

"Great," Monica replied. "I feel fine. I just gotta wash my hair."

"Are you sure you're better?"

"Why not?" Monica snapped. "I feel like a million dollars."

"Okay," said Cassie, going along with her. "Want me to wait while you wash your hair? Then we can go down to breakfast together."

"Fine," Monica said. "Fine."

As Monica padded into the bathroom, Cassie sank into a chair. She heard the water go on in the shower.

Monica spent a long time in the bathroom and finally emerged wearing a bathrobe and with her damp hair wrapped in a towel. She sat on the edge of the bed.

"Do you think you could just work with Kate today?" she asked weakly. "I guess I feel pretty rotten after all." She lay back on the bed.

"Then you definitely shouldn't work. Can't work!"

"Yeah, I think if I have just one more day of rest I'll be okay."

"Sure," Cassie said to soothe. She intended to get a doctor for Monica and right away, too. "That sounds reasonable to me. Don't worry about a thing."

"You're a peach," Monica said as she pulled the covers over her. Then she added, "What about Doug?"

"I'll go tell him that you're sick. Need anything while I'm out?"

"No," Monica replied. "I'll just call room service and order a gallon of orange juice."

"Okay, then," said Cassie. "I'm off."

As Cassie hurried out, she glanced around the courtyard. There was no sign of Doug. Checking her watch, she realized that he was probably down at breakfast. She was relieved she'd been right when she saw him eating with Barry and Kate. She rushed over to them.

"Doug," she said, "I think we've got a little problem."

He looked up at her. Cassie instantly recognized that fanatic expression that he wore when he thought there was a lot of work to be done.

He banged down his knife and fork. "Just take care of it. Whatever it is."

"I wish I could, but I don't see what I can do about it."

"All right. What's wrong?"

"Monica's sick."

"What do you mean she's *sick?*" he shouted.

Cassie spoke in a soothing tone of voice, trying to calm him down. "Didn't you notice that she seemed a little out of sorts last night?"

"Not really," he said curtly. "I remember her saying something about feeling tired. That's all."

Cassie looked at him incredulously. She wondered if he was intentionally being difficult or if he was so absorbed in his own world that he really hadn't noticed how pale and weak Monica had looked the night before.

"Well anyway," she said, "she feels awful now."

"She picked a dandy time," Doug said sarcastically.

"I don't think she did it on purpose," said Cassie, as she tried to keep her irritation from showing in her voice.

Doug put down his napkin and stood up. "I'd better

go and have a little chat with her. Where is she?"

"In her room. In bed."

"Come with me."

Doug was angry all right. And Cassie was amazed. His insensitivity bordered on the inhuman. They reached the sick woman's room and he rushed in.

Weakly, Monica propped herself up on one elbow. "Hiya, Doug."

"I hope you're not serious about this," he replied.

Monica looked confused. "Huh?"

"We can hardly afford to have you sick," he said.

"I know. I'm sorry. But it just sort of...uh.... happened."

"Are you sure you're ill? Maybe it's just in your head?" He studied Monica intensely.

"I don't think so," she said cautiously. "But maybe."

"Could you try to work today?"

Monica looked at Doug skeptically. "Gee," she said. Then she looked over at Cassie.

Cassie didn't know what to do to placate Doug. He was impossible! "I decided I could work with just Kate today," she said finally.

"Oh, you did, did you?"

"That way we won't lose a day," Cassie continued calmly in the face of his anger.

"You seem to be right on top of things, aren't you Cassandra?" Doug sneered.

"I'm just trying to be a productive professional," she said.

"But you don't *decide* anything around here and you don't give the orders."

"I wasn't—"

"I give the orders," said Doug. "And when I say something, you women jump."

Doug glared at Cassie. She returned his stare without

flinching and at last his eyes swung away from hers and around to the bed.

"What do you say, Monica? Want to get up and at 'em?" he asked.

Monica made a face and sat up. "I don't know how much good I'm going to do you guys."

"You let us worry about that," Doug said.

"Doug, this is crazy," Cassie said quickly.

"This isn't your business."

"Of course, it is," Cassie said. "Monica's my friend and she can't work because she's sick."

"She's not sick," said Doug.

Cassie was flabbergasted. She wanted to rage at him. Instead, she took a firm grip on her emotions and said, "Let's look at it from a practical point of view. If Monica works today, she might get sicker. Then you would have an even longer wait before she could work. Besides, we probably wouldn't get any shots we could use today anyway. Monica simply doesn't look any better than she feels."

"You'd better get some shots we can use," Doug said angrily. "It's your job to get good pictures. You damn well better do it."

"Don't be silly. If Monica's not feeling well, it's not going . . ."

Doug cut Cassie off. "I'm sorry we don't have a large enough budget to wait until you are suitably inspired, Cassandra. On this job, you're going to have to photograph what I tell you to, when I tell you to do it."

"Oh, knock it off, Doug," said Cassie angrily. "I can't work with somebody when she's ill. It's just not right."

"You're working for me. You do what I say."

Cassie shook her head. "I'm not going to go along with you."

"Nor am I," came a deep sonorous voice.

Whirling around, Cassie looked at Jack, who was leaning casually against the door, as though he'd been there for quite some time. Cassie couldn't help wondering how much he'd overheard.

"Really, Doug," Jack said. "This isn't a slave labor camp. If the young woman is ill, she'll have to take time off until she's better."

Doug glared, but didn't seem to be as eager to assert himself with the man as he had been with Cassie. Nevertheless, it was quite clear that Doug didn't like to be challenged.

"I'm in charge here," he muttered.

"That's true," Jack said smoothly. "But I don't think you'll get very far without a guide."

"You wouldn't dare."

"Consider it done!" Jack said calmly. Cassie was full of admiration for Jack's ability to handle crises so calmly. Doug was subdued and Jack coolly walked over to Monica's bedside and plunked down a first aid box. "Monica, I'm going to have to take your temperature."

Monica started feebly. "Oh no you don't!"

Jack stroked a clean, damp lock of hair off Monica's forehead. He had that tender expression on his face, the expression he'd worn when he'd saved the little gazelle. Cassie was surprised to realize that she watched for that kindly look to come into Jack's eyes and was comforted when she saw it.

"Monica, you're going to let me take your temperature," Jack said insistently.

"Do I have to?" Monica asked in a childlike whimper.

"You do," Jack replied. At this, Monica meekly opened her mouth for the thermometer. Jack patted her hand, then checked his watch.

As Jack gave the model a comforting smile, Cassie's emotions spun. There was no doubt that Jack seemed to care about Monica. Could he be falling in love with her?

Cassie felt Doug's eyes on her back and turned. He was glaring malevolently at her as though Monica's illness—or worse—were all her fault.

"Monica's temperature is a hundred and two," Jack announced solemnly.

"Gee whiz," Monica said.

"Cassie," Jack said, "There's a Dr. Sellers who's a guest here. He agreed to take a look at Monica, if I thought it was necessary. Would you mind getting him?"

"No. No, of course not. Right away," Cassie said, and wondered as she ran out of the room if Jack had noticed how choked her voice was.

Chapter Seven

CASSIE HAD BEEN too upset to eat much the day before and now her stomach was gurgling furiously, demanding food. She went to the long buffet table and helped herself to eggs, bacon, ham, Danish pastry, and fruit. She rounded off the meal with a huge, steaming cup of coffee. When she turned to take her spoils over to a table, she found herself face to face with Doug.

He looked at her, then at the heaping tray of food. "My goodness, Cassandra, one could certainly say you were eating enough to keep a bird alive...also a cow, a couple of horses, a gaggle of geese, and a small hippo. Where are you planning to put it all?"

"I'm starved. I didn't eat much yesterday and I must have burned off a million calories."

"You should have joined us for dinner," Doug said with a grin. "I had everyone in stitches with my stories."

"I'm sure you did," Cassie said. Then she added, "Let's sit down and eat. It's torture to stand here just holding all this food that smells so wonderful."

They sat down at a table together. Cassie wolfed down a good portion of her meal before she spoke again.

"How come you're in such a good mood?" she asked Doug.

"Am I?" he asked.

"You're grinning from ear to ear. Usually when you're working you don't smile much and you haven't smiled at all since Monica became ill."

"She's better," Doug said with a Cheshire cat smile.

Cassie's eyes widened. "Already?"

"The doctor says it's one of those short-duration flu things. He wants her to have a couple of days of bed rest just as a precaution, but right after—bright and early—I'm putting her to work."

"So that's why you look so happy."

"That's part of it," Doug said. "I've been doing a little thinking... since there was no shooting possible," he added bitingly.

"Oh?" Cassie tried for a casual tone, "any interesting conclusions?"

"Yeah. I decided that life's too short not to go after what you want. No more hanging back for me. I'm going to have a lot of things I want and that's all there is to it." He looked at her pointedly.

Cassie felt terribly uncomfortable. Here was another cat and mouse game from Doug to contend with and she didn't like it one bit. She decided to nip this particular flowering right in the bud. She popped up and slapped him playfully on the shoulder. "Glad you're getting it all together. Now I think I'd better run see Monica," she said. "Got to keep up her spirits if she's to make that fast recovery and keep the project on schedule. Right?"

She almost grinned at Doug's astonished expression and gave away her game, but she restrained herself in time and ducked her head. Then she grabbed a Danish pastry and bolted out of the room, calling an airy goodbye over her shoulder.

"Monica," Cassie called as she knocked at the model's door, "may I come in?"

"Sure," came the reply.

Cassie opened the door, walked in, and then stopped dead in her tracks. She had expected to see Monica sitting primly in bed sipping orange juice. Instead, there was the normally fastidious model sloppily devouring a very ripe piece of papaya. Monica wiped the juice from her chin and grabbed another piece of fruit from a heaping tray on her bedside table.

On the other bed were Kate and Jack. Jack lay with his head at the foot of the bed and his feet propped up against the headboard. Kate was sitting next to him feeding him grapes.

"We're having a Roman orgy," Monica announced.

Jack turned to see who had come in and smiled sheepishly at Cassie. A teasing glint appeared in his eyes. "Ah! Ms. Dearborn! I see you brought me a treat."

Remembering suddenly that she held the Danish pastry she'd taken from the dining room, Cassie asked dubiously, "Do you really want this?"

"Actually I had a different treat in mind," Jack said with a grin. "I realize that you owe me a favor, but I hardly think a mere cinnamon bun is adequate payment."

"What'd Cassie do?" Monica asked.

"Asked Jack to keep his wisecracks to himself," Kate said.

"And just generally stop being such a nuisance, I bet." Monica winked at Jack and clapped her hands together. "Let's all think of Cassie's punishment for being so mean to darling Jack."

"No, no, no," he said. "Ms. Dearborn herself has to decide how to repay me."

"Maybe for a starter she could take over grape duty," said Kate as she dropped a small green grape into Jack's mouth.

"No!" Cassie cried quickly, too quickly she thought.

"Oh, come on," pleaded Kate. "I'm getting hungry watching everybody eat."

"Surely Jack is capable of feeding himself," Cassie said tartly.

"We've made a rule that the men have to be hand fed," said Monica. Then she patted a place beside her on the bed. "Don't worry, Jack. I'll take care of you."

Suddenly, Cassie felt herself flushing with embarrassment. There was something so humiliating about seeing Jack go from her, to Kate, to Monica. Fighting the urge to go over and slap him, Cassie backed toward the door.

"I've got to go," she stammered.

"So soon?" Kate asked.

"She doesn't like our Roman orgy. It's obvious," Monica said with a giggle.

Cassie's blush deepened. "No, it seems fine. I just forgot to go over some stuff with Doug." Quickly, she hurried out of the room. But she froze after closing the door behind her.

Once outside, she couldn't decide where to go. She didn't dare walk back to the lounge to talk to Doug. She knew just where that would lead. He would start making covert sexual overtures to her. Then when she told him to stop he would pretend that he hadn't really meant what he said or he'd get angry and threatening. The very thought of going through those games made Cassie feel exhausted.

The only other people she could talk to were Max, Jill, and Barry. However, Barry had been cold to her ever since the day that she'd accidentally spilled coffee on his favorite jeans. Max and Jill were nice enough, but they were so absorbed with each other that they didn't really want anyone else around.

Just then, Cassie heard some giggles coming from Monica's room and heard Monica say, "I don't want to play charades, you guys! I'm terrible at it!" There was more laughter. Cassie bolted away and hurried to her own room. She locked the door and threw herself down on the bed.

Rolling over she stared up at the ceiling. Her eyes were stinging with tears. But the tears just stayed there, not brimming over, merely trembling on the lashes and blurring her vision. Damn! She wasn't even good at crying!

She felt terribly alone, as though life were going on all around her and she was the only one left out. Of course she could have stayed with Monica, Kate, and Jack, could have played at those games with them. She also could have been with Doug playing another kind of game. Yet, Cassie knew she still would have been alone even though she had their company.

What she wanted was to feel close to someone, really close. She hadn't really had that feeling since the early days of her marriage. She missed the feeling of being really in touch with another person, of trusting that person.

It seemed strange that she would be missing that feeling now. After all, she hadn't been close to Larry for several years and she'd managed to get along fine. Suddenly, here in the middle of Africa, she was longing for companionship.

Then Cassie realized that she felt the way she did because of Jack. There had been a moment when he'd told her to stop fighting him and she'd felt herself responding to him unquestioningly. In that brief encounter she had felt close to a man again. She remembered that she'd actually sensed that Jack cared for her and she could trust him.

Of course, she realized now that she couldn't trust him. She knew that he was the kind of man who flirted with any attractive, available woman. Yet he had awakened something in her. It was a shame that he wasn't a different kind of man. There certainly were qualities about him that she found attractive, but she knew she had to avoid falling for another ladies man—no matter how much he tempted her senses.

For the rest of that day, Cassie kept to herself. She wandered around the game park lodge alone. When she'd explored every corner of the place she went back to her room. There she wrote postcards to her family in Ohio and did a little reading. By the time dinner was ready, she was feeling bored and restless. However, she still wasn't ready to seek out the company of the others. Instead she decided to have the kitchen fix something that she could take back to her room.

As she stood in the kitchen doorway waiting for the cook to pack her a supper of cold cuts and fruit, Cassie heard a familiar sound, the low, haunting melody of Jack's whistle. At first she froze when she heard it. Then as the sound came closer, she shrank back behind the kitchen doorway hoping that he wouldn't notice her.

"I see you're lying in wait for me," Jack said as he broke off whistling. He was standing in the kitchen doorway staring at her. "You look like some sleek, marvelous cat who's waiting to pounce on her prey."

"Wrong," replied Cassie. "Just a hungry photographer waiting for supper."

"Eating in your room then?" asked Jack.

Cassie nodded.

"Why don't you join us in Monica's room?" suggested Jack. "I think she could use the company."

"I doubt that," said Cassie bitingly. "You and Kate seemed to be keeping her amused. I think I'd be intruding."

"Not at all," said Jack. "I think Monica was hurt that you didn't stay with us this morning."

"I wasn't in the mood."

"Well, it's a bit wearing for Kate and myself, too. But after all, Monica is sick."

Cassie studied Jack's face. Again, she saw that look

of tender compassion. She found herself sighing involuntarily.

"What is it?" asked Jack.

"I don't know," said Cassie. "I guess I just don't feel like going into Monica's room and goofing around all day. I'm sorry she's sick and I wouldn't mind spending some time with her alone. But, I just can't handle the other stuff."

"That's fair enough," said Jack. "And I must agree that the 'Roman orgy' was a bit silly."

Just then the cook came to hand Cassie her supper. She signed for the meal and then turned back to Jack. "Tell Monica that I'm glad she's feeling better."

"Of course," he said with a gallant half-nod, half-bow.

As she walked away, she could feel his eyes on her. Her skin flushed hot with embarrassment, but without looking back, she turned the corner and was safe from his gaze.

Cassie fell asleep early that night and woke just before dawn the next morning. She wasn't tired so she got up and put on her jeans and a pale blue cotton blouse. It was still chilly so she wrapped herself up in a big Spanish shawl and went outside.

Just as she was crossing the courtyard to the lounge she heard a voice whisper her name. She turned around, but didn't see anyone.

"Cassie!" hissed the voice again. "Over here!"

Hearing a finger tapping on glass, Cassie looked into the rooms that faced onto the courtyard. There was Monica peering through her window. Cassie crossed over to her.

"I feel so restless," Monica said without any greeting at all.

"Me too."

"I was ready to go back to work yesterday, but the doctor said no. I think I would have gone stark raving crackers if Jack hadn't stuck around to entertain me," Monica said with a slight smile. Then she added, "And Kate was a lamb, too. She was a barrel of laughs."

Cassie felt guilty that she'd been so inattentive. She blushed and looked down at the ground.

"Hey," said Monica brightly. "I've got a brainstorm. Want to hear it?"

"Sure," Cassie replied.

"Let's work."

"Now?"

"Yeah," said Monica. "Doug will be as pleased as a cat who just ate a parrakeet when he wakes up and sees us slaving away."

"It might be nice to just do a little work on our own," said Cassie thoughtfully.

"You're darn right it will," said Monica. "I'll just take my hair out of these dumb curlers and put on my makeup. You get your camera stuff."

"Terrific," said Cassie. She took a few steps toward her room, then she turned back. "I almost forgot. What about your wardrobe?"

"It's already here," Monica said without explanation, and disappeared into her room. Cassie went off and got all of her camera equipment together. By the time she got back, the model was ready.

"That was quick," Cassie said.

"It's because I'm so restless," Monica said. "It makes me speedy. Where do you want to shoot?"

"Let's start in the garden out back."

As they started down the path toward the garden, Monica squeezed Cassie's arm. "Boy, do I have news for you, kiddo."

"Oh yeah?"

"I'm in the throes of el supremo grand passion. Real romance."

"Oh," Cassie said flatly.

"By the time we're ready to leave I'm going to be Mrs. Jonathan Barton-Hyde."

"You mean Jack actually asked you to marry him?" Cassie cried. She wondered if she ought to warn Monica that only a few days ago Jack had tried to make love to her.

Monica looked at Cassie irritably. "Well, you don't have to sound so shocked and weird. I mean, I'm not *that* bad a catch. In fact, I'm pretty good-looking."

"That's not what I meant," said Cassie hastily. "Jack just doesn't strike me as the marrying type. He's a bit of a flirt."

"Jack?" said Monica incredulously. "He's just a pussycat. He's really shy."

"The man is hardly shy. He was flirting with both you and Kate at your Roman orgy! I saw him."

"Honestly, Cassie, don't you know anything? Kate doesn't count, she's engaged."

"Now who's being naive?" Cassie retorted. "Do you think that will make any difference to a man like Jonathan Barton-Hyde?"

"Cassie," Monica said. Her voice was suddenly serious. "You have the guy all wrong. You've had him wrong from the beginning when you tried to get him ousted."

"I don't think so."

"And you know what's even worse?" Monica said with an angry flush on her cheeks. "You really depressed me like crazy. Here I was all excited about trapping Jack for a trip up the aisle and you start telling me how awful he is."

As Monica turned away with a pout, Cassie lifted her camera and snapped a picture.

"Cassie!" Monica protested, but with the faintest trace of a smile. "You know that wasn't fair!"

"I suppose you're right," said Cassie as she snapped off another shot. "It wasn't fair to take the picture without warning and it wasn't fair to criticize Jack like that. I'm sorry."

"Okay. You're forgiven," Monica said. "Let's get to work."

With that, she jumped into the air and grabbed a branch. She hung from the branch like a circus performer hangs from a trapeze. She chinned herself once, then dropped and continued down the path.

"Do that again," Cassie called.

"Huh?"

"Hang from the tree like that. It's the perfect pose for that little red shorts outfit."

Grabbing hold of the branch, Monica grinned at Cassie. "If these shots make me look like a chimpanzee, I'll . . ."

"You'll what?"

"I don't know." She laughed and Cassie clicked off another picture. "Now admit it to me," Monica continued. "Admit that Jack is handsome."

"Hey, I'm no fool," Cassie said. "I think he's one of the most gorgeous men I've ever seen." She was about to add that it was those same good looks that gave him the idea that he could use women in whatever way he liked.

"Boy," said Monica. "When I get that guy over to Paris, I'm going to have him cut his hair and make him buy some really slick designer clothes. Then you are going to see a Greek god. I mean, that man is going to look yummy."

"He looks fine without all the trimmings."

"But I like my men to have some style."

"U-mm-m," Cassie murmured, not knowing what to say for the moment.

"Oh, Cassie, I don't know. It would be so fantastic to be married to a man like him. We'd get a condo in Paris on the Rive Droite..." Monica paused for a moment. "Or maybe it's the Rive Gauche I like. Anyway, one of those Rives. And we would eat out at Three Star restaurants every night. And our children would go to exclusive Swiss boarding schools."

Cassie nibbled at her lower lip. Poor Monica and her fantasy life. "What about Africa?" she asked, trying to force some reality to intrude on the model's daydream.

"I guess we'll have to come back here to run Jack's business. But that's okay. I kind of like it here. Besides Africa is pretty 'in' right now, so it will be fun."

"You don't want to stay here full time?"

"Not really." Letting go of the tree branch, Monica landed gracefully on the ground. "Let's find a new pose. I'm tired."

"What about over by those flowers?" Cassie suggested.

"Yeah, terrific." Monica struck a very dramatic pose and Cassie quickly snapped off a couple of shots.

"That's nice, Monica," she said.

Monica sighed.

"What are you thinking?"

"Oh about Jack, as if you need to ask," replied the model. "I get so scared though sometimes. I wonder if he'll get up the nerve to ask me. He's had an awfully hard time with women, you know."

"Jack?" Cassie said incredulously.

"Yeah, sure."

"I would think the only problem that man would have with women would be trying to keep the more aggressive ones at a safe distance," Cassie said dryly.

"You've got to stop talking about him like that," Monica protested. "You make him sound like he's some sort of male version of a vamp or floozie or something."

Cassie didn't say anything. She couldn't. All she

could do was remember the touch of Jack's lips and hands. He had the touch that could drive women mad. She didn't see how Monica could fail to recognize that.

"See, Jack's a real gentleman," Monica said. "That's one reason I like him. He doesn't go rushing into the sex stuff. He treats you like a lady."

Cassie almost dropped her camera. "Jack?" she said incredulously.

"No," said Monica sarcastically, "I was talking about Doug. Of course I meant Jack."

Quickly, Cassie looked into her camera lens so that Monica wouldn't notice her surprise. "That's a nice pose," she said. "I'll take a couple like that."

"This?" asked Monica, who was actually standing there scratching.

Cassie felt her skin get even hotter with embarrassment. "No, the one before."

As Monica fell into another pose, Cassie continued to snap away though her concentration wasn't what it should have been. She kept thinking about what Monica had said about Jack treating her like a lady. Could it be that he wanted sex from her but *not* Monica? Impossible! He'd encouraged her to lose herself in a sensual whirlwind and she shuddered when she remembered how persuasive his caresses had been. Damn! She'd ruined the shot. She gulped air and got steady of hand once more and continued to click away until finally a voice penetrated.

"Cassie!" Monica was saying. "Gee whiz! I mean, do I need a bullhorn or something to get your attention?"

Cassie looked up at Monica blankly. "What?"

"I asked you if I should go put on another outfit."

"Oh, right. You may as well."

"I think I'll put on that red and gold caftan next," Monica said. "Thinking about a rosy future makes me want to wear bright colors."

"I'll go back to the room with you," Cassie volunteered.

As they fell into step, Monica sighed again. "Oh boy," she said. "I just can't stop thinking about him. Would Tahiti be a nice place for a honeymoon?"

"Sure."

"I want to go somewhere real sexy and exotic."

Cassie stopped and put a detaining hand on Monica's arm. "You really think you're going to be able to get him to propose?"

"Sure," Monica said. But Cassie detected uncertainty in the model's face.

They walked along in silence for a while.

"As near as I can tell," Monica said. "There's only one thing holding him back."

"Oh?"

"And that's the first Mrs. Jonathan Barton-Hyde. If I ever meet that woman, I'll strangle her."

Cassie looked at Monica incredulously. "Jack was married?"

"Oh boy, was he married." Monica rolled her eyes.

"Really? What happened?"

"Oh, it was just one of those dumb things." They reached her room and Monica unlocked the door. "It's really a drag. I'll tell you all about it as soon as I get into that dress."

Cassie waited anxiously as Monica changed. She was eager to hear about Jack's marriage.

"How do I look?" asked Monica as she came out of the dressing area. She whirled around in the exquisite red and gold silk caftan with matching red and gold silk cord sandals. She had pulled her hair up on top of her head. The effect made her look like some sleek, exotic princess.

"Perfect," Cassie replied. Then she added with admiration, "You have the best eye for clothes."

"You look nice, too," Monica offered politely as she glanced at Cassie's jeans and blouse. "That's a neat shirt."

Cassie just shrugged. Even though it was a nice blouse with some beautiful hand embroidery, her clothes didn't begin to compare with Monica's. It would be foolish to pretend that they did or that she could ever look so good in the model's wardrobe."

"Anyway," Cassie said, trying to hide her eagerness, "you were saying something about Jack being married?"

"Oh that," Monica said as they walked down the path to the garden. "Poor baby got married when he was only twenty years old." Then she added with a giggle, "And only stayed married until he was twenty-two or -three."

"Why?"

"Oh, I guess she was just awful."

"According to Jack," Cassie interjected with a warning note in her voice. "Maybe her side of the story is different."

"Jack doesn't say bad stuff about her. But boy, you can sure read between the lines."

"What was she like?"

"Oh, he says she was real beautiful, thick brown hair, green eyes, the whole bit. I guess she was some sort of English aristocrat, related to one of those dukes or earls, you know the type. He says she was really smart, too."

"How'd he meet her?"

"They were studying animal husbandry at one of those fancy, English universities. Isn't that a weird thing to study?"

Cassie shrugged. "You know Jack and animals."

"Yeah," Monica said wistfully, "he's really cute when he's explaining stuff about elephant stampedes and everything."

Cassie nodded.

"I bet you'll just never guess how the marriage broke up," Monica said as she fell into a very theatrical pose.

"How?" Cassie clicked off the shot.

"Well," Monica said in her best gossipy tone of voice, "it all started when he caught her fooling around a couple of times. He found out that she was lying about all this stuff in their personal life. You know, saying she was going to visit a girlfriend and then going somewhere else to sleep with some guy."

"It hardly seems that Jack has the right to criticize her for that," said Cassie huffily. "I'm sure he had a few affairs of his own."

"Well, it's different for men, Cassie. We've discussed that already."

"Not in my book. If he was seeing other people, then he had no right to end the marriage just because his wife was doing that, too."

"Well, maybe he wasn't," said Monica with a shrug. "After all he was just a very young man. Maybe he was really trying to have a perfect marriage."

"Maybe," said Cassie thoughtfully.

"But the fooling around wasn't what ended it," continued Monica. "It was her lying. She was a compulsive liar."

"Really?"

"Yeah, and it was with the sex stuff that he first noticed that she lied."

"I didn't know that honesty was so important to Jack."

"Are you kidding? He's awful straight-laced about all that morals stuff. He really was embarrassed when he found out that she was lying to his family and friends all the time. Then she had some kind of car accident, one of those hit-and-run things. They traced it back to her and she tried to lie her way out of it. Jack was furious because a little kid was hurt and she didn't seem to care."

"And that's why he left her?"

"I guess it was the last straw or something. He was kind of funny about talking about it. Kate and I really had to pump him to find out what we did."

"So you think he hasn't proposed—to you or anyone else—because he was hurt so much the first time?"

"You bet," said Monica. "But I'll get him once he realizes that I won't give him a hard time."

"And you think it's just a matter of time?"

She nodded.

"Oh, Monica," Cassie wailed, about to launch into a little speech to bring the woman woman back to reality. But she was hushed by Monica who said, "Look! Jack."

Following the direction of her gaze, Cassie saw him coming toward them.

"Cassie, you don't think he heard what we were saying, do you?" Monica asked in a frantic whisper.

"He's too far away."

"He better not have," Monica muttered through a tight smile. Then throwing back her head, she waved. The wind caught her dress and blew it softly around her.

Quickly, Cassie snapped off a picture. As she did, she couldn't help thinking how perfect Moncia looked. She stood humbly and a little jealously to the side, as the model hurried to meet Jack.

He looked up when he saw her coming. "You're just the person I've been looking for."

"Me?" said Monica with a rather posed-looking blush.

"Yes," Jack replied. "Doug practically went berserk when you weren't in your room this morning. Why don't you hurry back to your sickbed before he turns an even less becoming shade of purple?"

"So you were just looking for me to please Doug?" Monica complained, with her sexiest pout. "I thought you might be looking for me because *you* wanted to see me."

"Monica, I'm always glad to see you. You know that," said Jack politely. "And you look very charming as usual."

"Thank you," Monica said. "You can tell Doug that I've been in wardrobe and I've been shooting with Cassie for the last hour or two, so he can just keep his socks on."

"Where is Cassie?" he asked. "I was just going to look for her."

"I'm right here," said Cassie from where she stood by the edge of the path.

Jack looked up in surprise. "Oh yes, so you are. Well, I'll just tell Doug that you two have been madly at work. And that Monica has to rest now."

Monica hooked her arm through Jack's. At first, this gesture seemed to startle him. Then he smiled at her. Turning around, he offered his other arm to Cassie.

"Ms. Dearborn?" he said. "Shall we escort this lady home?"

Cassie looked at the arm held out to her, then at Jack's face. All she could think was that she didn't want to be led anywhere with Monica on one arm and herself on the other like a couple of the great white hunter's game trophies.

"No, thank you," she said as she backed away. But Jack seemed a little insulted or disappointed. "The path just isn't wide enough for the three of us," Cassie explained hurriedly. "I'll tag along behind."

But as she followed them, she couldn't help feeling odd as Monica put her head against Jack's shoulder and laughed at a remark he made. She felt silly . . . and very much alone.

Chapter Eight

"CASSANDRA!"

Looking up from her book, she saw Doug. He was holding up a set of keys and grinning. And the grin shocked her. What was he up to now? He'd been in another foul mood the day before. He had had Cassie photograph Kate while Monica was in bed. They had been awful hours during which he screamed like a maniac at everyone. When he couldn't find anything for them to do he'd cursed and then paced frantically around the lodge while everybody else bent over backward to keep out of his way.

Doug shook the keys and they jingled pleasantly. "I know. You're speechless."

Cassie realized she'd been staring and tried to cover for herself. "I suppose I was. I couldn't help wondering what made you smile."

"Guess!"

"Because Monica's better and we were working a while ago."

Instantly, Doug's face darkened, signaling that she'd said just the wrong thing. She hoped that he wouldn't start screaming and pacing again.

"I don't have any luck on this trip," said Doug bitterly. Then he looked Cassie in the eye and added, "Do I?"

He seemed to be accusing her, implying that if she'd gone to bed with him this whole thing with Monica would have been a lot easier for him to bear—or would never have happened. Cassie didn't reply. She just looked him in the eye.

Doug went on. "That idiot Barton-Hyde raised hell just a while ago when I called on Monica to talk about work. He was at the bedside enforcing a rest.

Quickly, Cassie looked away. She couldn't bear the thought of Jack at Monica's bedside, though she knew how irrational she was being.

"You know?" Doug said. "You were right."

"About what?"

"Jonathan Barton-Hyde. I should have got rid of him straight off."

"I thought you said we needed him!"

Doug jingled the set of keys in his hand. "I'm beginning to wonder if we do."

Cassie panicked at the thought of Jack leaving.

"Yes, I think we may just have to replace the most sought after, exclusive guide in East Africa," said Doug with a chuckle. "And I may just have to mention that fact in the magazine. It's a pity for poor Jack. But then, I suppose he can survive a little negative press."

Feeling her skin flush with anger, Cassie fought to control herself. Yet she knew she couldn't say anything. If she made an issue of it she would just reinforce his determination to hurt Jack. If she let the statement pass, Doug might forget it by the time he got back to New York.

Doug jingled the keys again. "The first noble experiment. You and I will go for a little ride in the game park without Jack."

"But that's against the rules!"

"Now Cassie, you've never been one to follow the rules."

"Listen," she said, "we're talking about two different things. I don't believe in following every stupid little social rule, that's true. But that doesn't mean that I don't follow safety rules. That rule about traveling in the game parks with a guide is there for a reason."

"The reason being to line Jonathan Barton-Hyde's pocket."

"I don't think he needs the money that badly," Cassie said dryly.

"Don't think he doesn't get paid a very pretty penny for taking us around. And what does he do for us really? By this time you know as much about the animals as he does. You can name all of those funny looking deer."

"I think he knows a little bit more about animals than I do," Cassie replied. Brilliant images flashed through her mind of the Thomson's gazelle.

"Look," said Doug, assuming a very sensible voice. "I'm going out in that little bus. Why don't you come along and keep me company?"

"I don't really think I should," she replied.

"I have permission to take the bus you know."

Cassie's eyes widened. "From Jack?"

"From the game park people themselves," Doug said proudly. Then he held up the keys that he'd been jingling. "How else do you think I got these?"

"Why did they give you permission?"

"Because I'm the editor of the magazine."

"But that hardly makes you an animal expert."

"You don't need to be out here. It's just like one big zoo."

"That's not what Jack says."

"Jack's got an ego problem. He likes to make the job sound tough so that he'll sound tough—and wise. He gets more women into bed that way. Come on," he continued. "Don't be a coward. The game park people say they let certain guests go alone all the time."

Cassie was on the horns of a dilemma and she felt trapped—as trapped as that little gazelle had been, but without a rescuer. There could be no rescuer except herself in this situation. Quite simply, she wanted to slug her nasty, arrogant boss or tell him off or both. And she wanted a successful finish to this assignment that could spell great success for her career. Doug was a petty tyrant and Cassie's conscience told her that she must oppose him. But he was also one of the fashion world's most powerful editors and her ambition dictated that she cater to him. Either course would cause her pain and she searched for a middle road.

"It'll be great! I'd do anything to shrug off this awful boredom, wouldn't you?" Doug asked and nudged her ambition.

"It is a bit dull," she agreed.

"Then what are you waiting for?"

"My camera," Cassie said brightly. "I've got to get my camera."

"Leave it," Doug said. "You've been working hard enough. Let's just go."

"Okay," she said.

As they bumped along one of the dirt trails that crisscrossed the game park, Cassie fretted about how fast Doug was driving. It was about twice the speed that Jack and the other drivers traveled and made the road seem rougher.

"Let's go a little slower," said Cassie. "That way we'll be able to see the animals better."

"These are just wildebeests and zebras though," Doug said petulantly. "I want to wait until we get to some good stuff."

"Good stuff?" she asked.

"Like lions," he said with a glint in his eye.

With a sigh, Cassie sat back in her seat. Obviously, Doug intended to do everything his way. She'd been foolish to imagine she might have any say in what they did. And suddenly the wild countryside seemed very threatening indeed.

Suddenly Doug shouted out gleefully. "Terrific! A rhino!" he yelled, waving his arm in excitement.

Cassie saw the creature off in the distance. It stood alone on the plain. The other animals seemed to be keeping a respectful distance.

"Let's get a little closer," Doug said overloud like an enthusiastic schoolboy.

"Okay," said Cassie. "But not too close. Remember Jack says they don't like to be crowded."

"'Jack says,' 'Jack says,'" Doug mimicked. "As if Jack were the Lord on High."

Doug turned off the dirt trail and drove across the plains toward the animal, stopping a reasonable distance away. With relief, Cassie noticed that it was about the same place that she judged Jack would have stopped.

The rhino's squinty little eyes peered in their direction.

"Pretty ugly son-of-a-gun," Doug muttered.

"I wonder what he's thinking."

Doug just grunted in response.

"He probably thinks we're being very audacious to come into his domain," Cassie mused.

"He's just jealous because we've got armor, too." Doug laughed as he knocked on the metal side of the little bus.

"Rhinos don't have armor. They have thick skin," Cassie said.

"Don't take that role of animal expert too seriously," Doug said in a cranky tone of voice. "I've had enough of that with Jack."

Cassie's lip curled in disgust, but she didn't say anything.

"Let's get a better look," he said pushing down hard on the accelerator before Cassie could do more than gasp, then mutter for him to stop. He didn't, of course, and she realized the worst all at once. Doug's stupidity and his envy of Jack caused him to behave like a lunatic in this situation. Cassie squeezed her eyes closed as the full force of the danger here hit her. She gripped the edge of her seat. Her palms were sweaty. She had to treat Doug very, very carefully or all was lost. "I don't think this is such a good idea," she observed mildly.

"Let me worry about that," Doug snapped, pulling up close to the rhino. "Now this is what I call getting a good look at this guy."

Looking into the rhino's beady eyes, Cassie was sure she could see pure hatred smoldering there. The animal lowered its head. Then it made threatening upward and sideward thrusts with its horn.

"Um . . . Doug," Cassie said, trying the soft, soothing approach again, "he looks like he's none too pleased with us. Let's get out of here pretty soon, all right?"

"Not until I get a look at his other side," Doug said.

"No! Don't!" she said urgently.

Ignoring her, Doug drove around the rhino, who kept turning to face them. The creature always kept his horn in the direction of the bus, poised—threateningly, Cassie was sure.

Her throat felt choked with fear, but Doug seemed still to be unaware of any danger.

"What if he comes after us?" she asked in a hoarse whisper.

"Don't be ridiculous," Doug scoffed.

He continued driving the minibus slowly around the rhino. The animal made thrusts with its horn more and more often.

"Look at that guy! Look at him!" Doug said. He seemed to be mesmerized by the animal, his power behind the steering wheel that permitted this closeness, the whole scene.

Suddenly, the rhino lowered his head. He backed up a couple of steps as though he were gathering power. Then he began to move ominously toward the bus with a lumbering, thundering stride.

"He's charging!" Cassie yelled.

Doug froze. The bus stopped.

With her quick athletic reflexes, Cassie pressed her foot down over his on the gas pedal. Just in time, the bus jolted wildly forward.

The rhino missed its target.

Cassie watched apprehensively as it dug its feet into the ground and stopped.

Doug wasn't really steering. He just sat numbly in the driver's seat. The bus moved across the plains out of control. Cassie tried to grab the steering wheel but she really wasn't able to drive leaning over Doug like that.

Another glance in the rear view mirror revealed that the rhino had turned and lowered his head as if to charge again. Doug was still paralyzed with fear.

"Move over!" she yelled to Doug.

He just sat there.

She elbowed him in the ribs as hard as she could. "Damn it! Move!"

Doug obeyed reflexively, it seemed to Cassie, and she slid into the driver's seat as he arced his body and flopped into the spot she'd just vacated. Not a moment too soon she gunned the engine and sped away from the charging animal.

The ground was rough and Cassie was afraid to drive the bus too fast. She glanced into the rear view mirror. At this speed the rhino was still dangerously close. She decided that she'd better accelerate.

Another glance at the mirror told her that the animal had lost some ground, but he was still pursuing. Just a little faster and she'd put enough space between them so that the rhino would have to give up the chase. She pressed down on the accelerator. She blinked at the mirror. The rhino seemed to be slowing his speed. He was getting discouraged. She felt jubilant!

And then there was a sharp jolt to the bottom of the bus. As she bounced in her seat, Cassie realized that something was dreadfully wrong. The bus's engine grew ominously still. They rolled forward powerlessly. She turned the keys trying to start the engine again. Futile!

"What'd you do? What'd you do?" Doug shrieked.

"I don't know," she said shakily. "It felt like we hit a stone or a tree stump."

"You should have watched where you were going!" he yelled.

As the bus slowed to a stop, Cassie looked around and saw that the rhino was gaining on them. He galloped forward eagerly.

"What are we going to do?"

"I don't know," Cassie said. "There doesn't seem to be anything we can do—except pray, Doug."

"Surely, that beast can't hurt us. The bus will protect us. It . . . it has to."

"Just pray. Sit here quietly and pray that animal leaves us alone."

The rhino came thundering over a rise. As he came closer to the stranded bus, he slowed down. For a moment, Cassie was sure he would pass them by. Then she saw the beast lower his head and knew her certainty for the forlorn hope it was. The rhino had only slowed to gather himself for the charge.

As she watched the animal coming toward them, Cassie braced herself in her seat. She heard the volume of the rhino's hoofbeats getting louder. Then she smelled the stench of the beast a moment before she felt the crash.

The creature had much more force than Cassie could ever have imagined. The small bus shuddered under its attack. The brunt of the blow hit against Cassie's door. She was thrown across the seat and landed on top of Doug. She could feel his body shaking underneath her and realized that he must be shaking, too.

"Are you all right?"

Doug nodded. "What about you?"

"Fine," she said. "Fine," she repeated as if she were trying to reassure herself.

Pushing her from him, Doug slid over on the seat and looked out Cassie's window to inspect the damage. "Oh my God!" he muttered.

"It's that bad?" asked Cassie.

Doug looked at the animal as if mesmerized and unable to answer her. The rhino had lowered its head and was facing the bus.

"It's going to come at us again," Doug said. He shrank back along the seat toward Cassie. She had an uneasy feeling that he wanted to crawl behind her and use her to shield himself.

As the rhino's powerful body crashed against the door, Cassie and Doug clutched at each other. The force of the blow threw him against her and she was crushed between his heavy body and the door.

She had closed her eyes tight, as though that might in some way protect her from the rhino's blow. Now as she opened them, she saw that the force of the creature's thrust had bent back the door on the driver's side. It gaped open . . . dangerously. Doug saw the open door a moment after she did.

"Close it quick!" he said to her fearfully.

"Can't," Cassie said. "It's dented. Get in the back. It can't reach us in the back."

As quickly as she said these words, Cassie wondered if they were true. And she wondered how long the small bus could survive the onslaught of the powerful animal.

Doug dived over the seat and into the back. As he did

his head banged hard into Cassie's. Once he was safe he pulled her after him, bruising her arm. She would have been a lot better off if she'd climbed over under her own power.

Through the open door, Cassie saw the rhino's head not ten feet away. Her heart was hammering in her chest. She wanted to scream at Doug for being such a fool and getting them into this mess. But she knew that would only make things worse and it certainly wouldn't get them out of this situation.

"What if he charges right up into the bus?" whispered Doug. "He'll kill us."

Cassie didn't reply. She kept her eyes on the rhino as he snorted menacingly. Surely, if he kept on attacking them like this, they would be seriously injured. She couldn't see how she could possibly protect herself. Maybe Doug was right. Maybe they would be killed.

Just then the rhino broke off its pacing and whirled toward the front of the bus. He took a few steps forward and butted it with his horn. It wasn't nearly as hard a blow as the first two. Cassie began to hope that the animal would get exhausted or bored and leave them alone. Unfortunately, the blow, light as it was, was enough to set the bus in motion and the movement seemed to enrage the rhino. His tiny eyes flashed with hatred again and he gathered himself for another lunge.

Doug grabbed Cassie's hand. His palms were pouring with sweat. He squeezed her fingers so hard they hurt.

As the rhino galloped toward them Cassie could only stare in terror. She had the vague sensation of something on the periphery of her vision, a cloud of dust perhaps. However, she was too focused on the rhino to give any thought to anything else.

Then she heard the crack of a gunshot. The rhino faltered in its stride, but kept coming. She heard another shot. The rhino staggered and slowed. Then he continued on relentlessly. He crashed into the bus with a force that sent Cassie flying across the seat.

The impact of the rhino's blow sent the bus speeding backward until it hit a rock and jolted to a stop. Pulling herself together, Cassie twisted in her seat to locate the rhino and look for whoever fired the shots.

She saw the animal walking around in a circle. Every few seconds he shook his head vigorously, yet his gesture wasn't as threatening as the jabs he'd made before. Now it seemed almost as though he were trying to clear water out of his ears. But he didn't seem to be wounded. Cassie was puzzled because she was sure that she'd heard two shots and seen the animal falter in its stride.

Looking around some more, she saw Jack. He was sitting in the jeep watching the rhino. He had a rifle poised across his knees. She was so relieved to see him that her first impulse was to lean out the window and wave. But his expression was very grim. He didn't look as though he would welcome that kind of a lighthearted greeting and she realized the inappropriateness of what she'd been about to do must have its source in shock.

In a flash, Cassie remembered that Doug had been anxious to show Jack that he wasn't as impressive as he seemed to think. How that had backfired and he'd been the one proved not only unimpressive, but a fool. She, too, was a fool! It seemed strange to experience the emotion of embarrassment, though, after being in terror for her life. She sighed on an insight. Instinctively she'd known that she was out of danger and that had precipitated the embarrassment.

"Is that Jack?" asked Doug quietly.

"Yes," Cassie said. Doug was leaning between the corner of the seat and the door. His eyes looked glazed. Cassie gasped. Drops of blood fell from his cheek onto his shirt.

"I'm bleeding," he said, looking down at the stain on

his shirt, apparently as shocked as Cassie.

"Shall I take a look?" she asked gently.

Doug nodded, then turned to show her the cuts. There was a scrape along his forehead and another one along the cheekbone. She couldn't tell how deep they were but she knew she ought to stop the bleeding. There was usually a first aid kit in the glove compartment. Keeping a cautious eye on the rhino, Cassie leaned into the front and opened the compartment. It was empty.

Cassie didn't know how she was going to bind the cuts at first. The only cloth she had were her own clothes. "Fool," she muttered, then she ripped off the sleeve of her shirt, folded it, and pressed it against Doug's head wound.

"The rhino," Doug said faintly.

Frightened, Cassie looked out the window only to see the rhino sink to its knees and then lie down. After it had lain there a few minutes, Jack slowly began to edge the jeep around toward them. He kept far away from the rhino and moved very slowly and carefully.

As he drew closer to the bus, Cassie could see his eyes. They looked cold and furious. His wild dark shaggy curls fell around his face in a way that made him look menacing, and his mouth was set in a harsh, unforgiving line.

Involuntarily, Cassie shrank back against Doug as Jack leaped out of the jeep. Her heart began to pound as he approached the back door of the bus. He looked almost as threatening as the rhino.

"Are you hurt?" he growled as he tried to open the back door.

Cassie was too numb to answer.

"I'm bleeding," was all Doug could say.

"Damn it! Are you all right, Cassie?" Jack cried. He used more force on the door but it was stuck. Enraged, he kicked at it with his bush boots. A metalic echo sounded through the bus.

"Don't!" cried Cassie, glancing fearfully at the rhino. Jack looked over at the animal, too, but it didn't stir. Then he noticed that the door on the driver's side was open. He raced around in a few long strides until he was glaring in at Cassie and Doug.

"Can you get over the seat?" he asked.

Cassie nodded.

Doug muttered, "I think so." Cassie couldn't believe how meek he was. She'd never seen him this docile.

He gestured for Cassie to climb over the seat first. That seemed a little ironic since he'd gone first when it was a matter of life and death. Once she was out of the bus, standing on the plain, Cassie felt her knees go weak. She tried hard not to let Jack see how shaken she was.

But he grabbed her arm and turned her around. Cassie knew that he was checking her over for wounds, but she felt as though he were handling her like a piece of meat. She glanced at his face, hoping to see that tender expression that she'd seen at Monica's bedside, but his look was cold and stern. She felt tears filling her eyes and she blinked them back.

"Are you sore anywhere?" asked Jack.

"My sides," she replied in a choked voice.

"Pull up your blouse," he commanded.

Cassie wanted to resist his order but she felt too weak. Jack ran a practiced hand over her stomach and ribs.

"Doesn't look too bad to me," he said coldly. "But we'll have the doctor check you out anyway." He turned his attention to Doug. "Let's see that," he said as he pulled Cassie's shirt sleeve off the cuts. "This doesn't look too deep."

"It's bleeding an awful lot."

"Head wounds usually do," Jack said shortly. "Let

me get you a decent bandage." He threw Cassie's shirt sleeve into the dirt and—oddly she thought—crushed it into the dirt with the heel of his boot.

He went to get his first aid kit out of the jeep, came back, and started to bind up Doug's scrapes. Finally, he spoke. "Now suppose you two tell me your excuses." It was obvious he was furious even though his fingers worked calmly on Doug.

Cassie didn't know what to say. She hated to accuse Doug of angering the rhino, even though that was the truth. "I don't know where to begin," she mumbled.

"You might start with why you took one of the tour buses without permission," Jack said icily.

Cassie glared at Doug, realizing he had lied about that, too.

Catching her look, Doug glanced away quickly. "It was my fault. I told Cassie that I had permission to go out by myself."

"And she believed you?" Jack asked archly. "Really Ms. Dearborn! I would have thought you were far too intelligent to fall for that line. You disappoint me."

Cassie wanted to shoot back a retort, but she didn't. After all, the man had just saved her life. She bit her lip and hung her head. She felt that in some way she deserved these insults since she'd been such a fool.

"She told me to slow down near the rhino, too," said Doug. "It's not her fault at all."

Shocked that he came to her defense, Cassie stared at Doug. It seemed odd that just when she'd branded him as utterly hopeless he did something almost noble. She'd half-expected him to try to blame the whole thing on her.

Jack didn't seem to be very impressed that Doug was trying to defend Cassie. "Then what's your excuse?" he asked Doug hostilely.

Doug regained a mite of his normal self. He shrugged

and grinned. "New York's a jungle. I figured I could handle anything after that. I was an idiot."

"You were worst than that," Jack said fiercely. "You could have gotten Ms. Dearborn killed along with yourself. It's one thing to be foolish with your own life, but quite another to endanger someone else."

"You're right. I'm sorry," Doug muttered.

"Sorry!" Jack sneered. "That's mild to say the least."

"How did you find us?" Cassie interjected.

"I discovered the bus was missing. Someone said they'd seen you leave in it. I've been out looking for you ever since. Fortunately, I happened to notice that rather ominous looking dust cloud," Jack said. Then he added wryly, "You're lucky the weather's been so dry lately. Otherwise I doubt if I could have found you in time."

Cassie was speechless.

"Here's Timothy," Jack said, nodding toward an approaching tour bus.

"Timothy?" Cassie said.

"I called him on the car radio right after I shot the rhino. I thought I might need help."

"Oh."

"He'll take you back to the lodge."

"What about you?" she asked anxiously.

"I'm going to stick around and make sure that our rhinoceros friend recovers from the tranquilizers."

"Then he's not . . ."

"Dead?" Jack finished. She nodded. "Of course not! He's just been stunned. But he will be dead if I leave him out here for the other animals to pick at."

Timothy, one of the Kikuyu drivers, pulled up alongside Cassie, Jack, and Doug.

"Take these two back to the lodge and make sure that the doctor who's staying there takes a look at them," Jack ordered to the other driver.

"Yes, Sir," Timothy replied.

Cassie turned to Jack. "Won't it be dangerous for you to be out here on your own?"

"It's not nearly as dangerous if you know what you're doing," said Jack pointedly.

Cassie nodded in mute embarrassment. She put a gentle hand on Jack's arm and looked directly into his eyes. "An inadequate word, Jack," she murmured, "but the only one I have in mind at the moment—*thanks*." Tears welled and she ducked her head, then darted into the tour bus.

Chapter Nine

BY THE TIME Cassie and Doug came out of the doctor's room, Barry, Max, Jill, and Kate had all gathered outside to wait for them.

"What's this about a rhino?" Barry asked.

"Timothy said something about your being attacked. Is that true?" Kate chimed in.

Max put a protective arm around Jill. "Maybe we should leave the women behind next time we go out into the bush. What do you think, Doug?"

Doug just laughed. "Hey, what's going on here? I feel like I'm at a press conference with all these questions."

Cassie could see that he was in his element, being at the center of attention. He seemed very pleased with himself, as he raised his hands to get the group to quiet down.

"Why don't we all go into the bar and have a drink? Then Cassie and I can tell you all the grizzly details."

"Monica's going to be pea green with envy when she finds out she missed this," Kate asserted.

"Serves her right for being sick," Doug replied with a vindictive gleam in his eye.

"That patch on your head, Doug," Barry said, pointing to the new bandage that the doctor had put on. "You didn't get gored there did you?"

"If I had, I certainly wouldn't be alive to tell about it!" Doug laughed.

Jill shuddered involuntarily.

"Come on, let's go to the lounge. Drinks on me," said Doug as he held out his hand to Cassie.

She shrank away from him. She knew that she just couldn't go into the bar and listen to Doug describe what they'd been through in that jovial guffawing manner. The experience was still too fresh and too frightening to hear it retold as a New York cocktail-party anecdote. "I'm just going to go to my room" Cassie said. "I think I need to lie down."

"You sure you don't want to join us?" Doug asked.

She nodded and turned away from the group before anyone had a chance to press her to stay. Once she was in the privacy of her own room, she quickly undressed and showered. Then she pulled a filmy pink cotton nightgown out of her suitcase. She put it on and looked at herself in the mirror. She looked very frail in the frothy, lacy negligee. It made her realize once again that her body would have been totally vulnerable to an attack by the rhino. If Jack hadn't arrived when he did . . . Cassie wouldn't even allow herself to complete that thought in her mind.

Anxiously, she looked around for something that would keep her mind diverted. Remembering the paperbacks that she'd brought from New York, she rumaged through her suitcase. She found one that looked as though it might be lively enough to keep her occupied. Settling into bed, she adjusted the lamp and began to read. But after an hour or so, she still hadn't managed to finish the first chapter. The words blurred, faded, were without meaning for her.

There was a knock on the door.

"It's not locked," she called.

The door swung open. "Jack!" Cassie exclaimed, drinking in the blue of his eyes as he stared at her from beneath his wild, dark curls. He must have come right in from the plains because his safari clothes were smudged with dirt. Her breath caught at the easy grace of his body and the power of his muscular frame. She felt a surge of excitement as he took a step into the room.

"What are you doing in bed?" he asked tersely.

"I just didn't want to deal with the others," she said hoarsely. "Why?"

"I was worried that you might be hurt."

"No, I'm fine," said Cassie. She waited apprehensively for the lecture that she was sure he was going to give her. However, he didn't say anything for the longest time. Finally, she couldn't stand it any longer and decided to force the issue. "I suppose you're furious."

"You did give me quite a fright," he said. With that, he stepped all the way into her room and closed the door behind him. Cassie froze, wondering what he was going to do next. He walked slowly toward her.

Jack moved like a powerful cat. He sat lightly on the edge of her bed and handed her a mug of hot liquid. Startled, because she hadn't even noticed he held anything in his hands, she accepted it.

"What's this?" she asked.

"It's a hot rum toddy. I thought it might be soothing after what you've just been through."

"Thank you," she muttered. She was deliciously aware of his nearness.

"Well?" he said raising an eyebrow. "Are you going to just sit there warming your hands on the mug? Or do you intend to drink a little?"

"Oh . . . right," she said. She took a sip and felt the warm liquid sliding all the way down to her stomach.

"Is that better?" he asked gently.

She nodded and took another sip. The warm liquor seemed to go directly into her bloodstream, for within moments her head felt lighter, her muscles relaxed.

Jack had just watched her silently, but now he spoke. "As I was saying, you gave me quite a fright."

"I suppose it wouldn't look very good for your business if a couple of your charges got themselves killed." Cassie's tone was light, teasing.

Jack's jaw clenched. "No joking matter," he said in a bitter voice. "That didn't happen, so let's not even mention anything like it."

"I'm sorry," Cassie said. And she truly was. "I shouldn't have said what I did, even in jest. You wouldn't have been responsible in any way. Doug and I were both very foolish."

"You mean Doug! Don't include yourself. I'll never forgive him for that trick he pulled on you. I don't know what I would have done to him if you'd been hurt."

Cassie's heart thumped erratically at his words. "You managed to get there. You..." She had been about to say that Jack had saved their lives, but she couldn't quite bring herself to utter the words. Part of the reason was that the phrase sounded corny to her ears. The more important part was that she felt almost threatened to say aloud that she'd been so close to death. And been saved... by Jack. He had a special power over her now and she feared it all of a sudden. It loomed like the slippery lip into an abyss. With the warm rum in her blood and Jack so close that she could hear his breath, the abyss yawned beneath her.

"What were you thinking?" he asked tenderly.

"Nothing," she stammered.

"No evasions. That was deep thought you were engaged in, my dear. There was an ominous little furrow between your brows." Jack reached out to stroke lightly at the wrinkle on her forehead. "Now what was it all about? I know I'm heavily involved in those deep ruminations."

At the moment all she could think of was his hand on her face and her crazy desire to take any consequences tomorrow if she could have Jack tonight. Nothing else mattered—the other women in his life, even Monica, his commitment to her or lack of it, nothing except her overwhelming need. "Jack, I'm—well, maybe I'm not myself tonight."

"No wonder," he said. He ran his hand along her jawbone and down her neck.

Her skin tingled where he touched her. She drew away ever so slightly to relish the sensation but his fingers pursued her, caressing her neck and shoulder. His hand stopped and rested lightly on her arm.

"*Too* confused right now, Cassie?" he murmured. "Too confused for this?"

"Why . . . why . . . what do you mean?"

Jack began hesitantly, "Because . . . well . . . you've been through a lot lately. Not merely with that rhino, but your professional and personal life, too."

Cassie stiffened. That same feeling of resistance she'd had to Jack in the beginning and so often since rushed back in on her. Tasting if fully she realized the resistance had altered, though, from the physical and somewhat emotional to . . . Yes, the real threat he posed was to her soul, her essential being. She shivered at her exquisite vulnerability in the face of this man and he clasped her shoulders tightly, as if he'd read her mind and knew she needed reassurance. Her eyes rose to his and the gentle concern she saw there made her feel as though her bones might dissolve. She simply couldn't deal with Jack's worming his way into her very heart like this and dropped her gaze.

"A divorce is one of life's biggest crises, isn't it, Cassie?" he asked softly.

She nodded mutely, thinking of his bad experience and, curiously, not of her own.

"At first it's the hurt and disappointment, the uncertain future to deal with—"

"Please, Jack," she cried.

"No, Cassie, let me finish. What I have to say won't hurt for long, if it hurts at all. It's really the sense of *failure* that is the torture divorce brings."

Her eyes flew to Jack's face, which looked drawn, abstracted now. He was so on target that she felt an uncanny sense of being part of him.

"Yes, failure," he went on, "and at two levels at least. There's the sense of failure about the actual tapestry of your interactions—could you have done more, stretched yourself more to meet the other's needs, tried harder, all that. But the other part of it is even more tormenting and destructive. Judgment. You question your judgment. Why did you make such a mistake in the first place, stick with it as you did, and will you make the same—or even a different, perhaps worse mistake next?" He clutched her urgently. "A big subject, Cassie, and I haven't done it justice at all. But I know you question your every reaction now and it's the major reason I asked if you were too confused for this."

A wave of appreciation for Jack's sensitivity washed over her. It was quickly followed by an even greater swell of desire, though. She wrapped her arms tightly around him, stroking the muscles of his back so warm through his safari jacket. "I'm *not* too confused," she managed to whisper.

At those words, Jack pulled her even closer. She felt the rush of breath from his lungs and then his hand slipping to her waist to press her body down, sliding her under him. She lay beneath him, chest and lips crushed against chest and lips, his weight, curiously, not hurtful but exciting. Oh, yes, the whole set of movements had been as natural as water flowing downhill and even now she felt as though she were floating.

Jack released her mouth to burrow his face in the curve of her neck. "My darling girl," he said over and over. The bedclothes were still between them, yet Cassie could feel his every muscle through all the fabrics separating them and her pulses clamored for his possession. His mouth was on hers again for a languorous, probing kiss that brought every fiber in her body to full life. His lips eased down her neck and back up to her earlobes.

"Damn—the—bedding," he muttered into her ear, between sensuous flicks of his tongue on the shell of her ear, "and damn our clothing, too."

She chuckled huskily. "What do you propose to do about it, sir?"

"Hmm-m, good question, my provocative lady." He laughed and suddenly Cassie felt cold and quite bereft. Jack was on his feet, towering above her next to the bed. Her brows rose in surprise. "Your lovely gray eyes look like the little gazelle's. Now, did I abandon him?" He laughed again and swooped down to kiss her as he tore the sheets away. Then his arms scooped her up and he was walking with her, never ceasing to ply her mouth with kisses. Cassie was dizzy with wanting, awash with excited curiosity—about what he intended to do, about the promises his passion held.

"Caveman," she breathed into his mouth, "where are you taking me?"

He put her on her feet and snapped on the bathroom light, then deftly reached behind the shower curtain and turned on the faucets. "To a water festival," he said in a voice deepened by desire, "and I propose we plan to shed my grime from the plains there along with all our inhibitions."

Cassie's breath went rackety and she sagged against him, weak with excitement. She slipped her hands between their bodies and began to unfasten the buttons on his jacket.

"I take it the proposition is acceptable," he muttered

low, with not a trace of questioning in his voice.

"More than acceptable," she said, stepping back and removing his jacket.

Slowly they alternated undressing each other, taking long moments to savor with eyes, hands, and mouths each exposed part of the other's body. And in the shower Cassie truly lost the last of her inhibitions with Jack as they soaped and stroked, rinsed and caressed, learning about the other, delighting the other. Cassie had never felt so free, gratified, and gratifying.

And when they returned to bed, dripping wet and desperate for fulfillment, Cassie was as unselfconscious as a child who hasn't yet learned about shame. Rejoicing in the muscled beauty of his body and her own ability to give pleasure, she lay atop Jack and let her tongue wander over his chest. She teased his flat nipples as he'd teased her rounded breasts and knew a wild new thrill at the moans she elicited from him. Then his hands were at work again, fingers exploring and exciting, until they were both unable to hold back a moment more.

Jack entered her with a delicious slowness that belied the urgency she knew that he felt as much as she did. She encouraged him to quicken his movement by the fast thrusts of her hips. They moved as one in frenzied heat, blazing together, crying out simultaneously at the scorching pleasure of their passion.

Cassie was awed by the heights to which she'd crested and overjoyed by each tender kiss Jack left against her temples, her hair, her shoulders as though worshipping her. They held one another gently, trembling a little before they became totally still.

"Cassie," Jack murmured, "that was perfect. Magnificent."

"Magnificent," she echoed and tightened her hold on him.

He propped himself on one elbow to gaze down on

her. "I'd anticipated a fine and lovely pleasure for us, darling woman, but not this magic." He shook his head as if astonished. "No, I never dreamed of . . . of so much magic between us."

Tears welled in Cassie's eyes as she savored his words which were as rich as the afterglow of his lovemaking. Indeed, the intensity of their pleasure in one another had been nothing short of magical. She pulled his head down to hers for a long, sweet kiss, and then folded herself into the curve of his body. "Thank you, Jack; thank you, my sensual magician." She breathed deeply, filled with a contentment she sensed Jack shared, and she knew utter peace.

They awoke in the night and made love again—more slowly, far less urgently than they had before. Jack's leisurely, infinitely patient yet vigorous exploration of all her senses brought Cassie to a shattering, utterly new and different peak of satisfaction.

Dawn light seeped into the room as Cassie bolted upright. She was covered with perspiration and the nausea of pure fright had made her mouth taste of bile. She'd had the most awful nightmare, so similar to ones she'd had when she'd first learned Larry was seeing other women. She was in a deep muck-filled lake with weeds dragging her to the bottom. She struggled to break free and surface, but was helpless against the green, slimy tentacles pulling at her legs. A man swam lazily above her, but would not look down and lower the saving hand.

The grip of the dream was still so powerful that she gasped and choked trying to suck air into her tortured lungs. The noise awakened Jack.

"Cassie, Cassie, dear girl, what's the matter?"

She turned a panic-stricken face to him. Oh, Lord, all of a sudden she understood. Because of the loss of love she'd suffered, she felt deep inside that to give away a part of herself was to tempt a destructive fate. And to give all of herself away as she had to Jack in the night was suicide. She gasped. Was there any truth really to all this? Need she fear the man who'd enfolded her this minute so protectively?

Jack murmured reassurances, then waited for her to find her voice.

"I...I don't trust...you," she faltered. "Or maybe it's myself I don't trust."

"Of course you don't trust me—or yourself. We don't know one another well enough. Can you be reassured to know that time is your answer, Cassie?"

She shook her head in bewilderment. "Time will tell, Jack? But we've had a number of unpleasant encounters so far and—"

"Monica?" Jack asked with an edge to his voice.

"Well," said Cassie. "When I found you flirting with both Monica *and* Kate all I could think about was how horribly fickle you were..." her voice trailed off.

"Strangely enough, this is what I had expected to say. You think there is something going on between me and Monica, don't you?"

"I'm sure there is," she replied levelly.

"Oh dear," said Jack with a heavy sigh. "I can't answer for Monica's feelings toward me, but I can tell you that I've never been the least involved. I have never made love to her."

Cassie looked up at him, startled.

"Oh, I think she's a nice enough person," said Jack. "I felt sorry for her a bit, particularly when she got sick and Doug behaved so abominably. Monica strikes me as a mixed-up, lonely woman. She seemed to need a lot of attention and I was trying to be kind. I never would have done that if I had realized that I might be ruining things with you."

"I see," said Cassie coolly, not quite daring to trust

him yet. "And what about that morning in Monica's room, with you and Monica and Kate?"

"First of all, my dear," Jack said, "there was hardly anything going on between myself and those women. We were there because she was ill and she'd asked us to keep her amused. I'll be the first to admit that we had gotten a bit silly and I was terribly embarrassed when you walked in."

"Jack, you make it all sound incredibly innocent," Cassie said guardedly. "And it may well have been for all I know. But, it honestly did look as though you were flirting up a storm with both of them.

Jack's color rose. "Well, I suppose I might have been." Then he hastily added, "With Kate, not with Monica."

"Why?" she asked in a challenging tone.

"A lot of reasons," he replied. "One was that Monica was developing a crush of sorts on me. I was paying a lot of attention to Kate, hoping that Monica would realize she wasn't anything special to me."

"What were the other reasons?"

"Those are a bit hazier in my mind, but they have something to do with you."

"With me?" she said incredulously.

"Yes, I'd always known I was terribly attracted to you. From that first moment when you came running into the hotel in Nairobi with your hair wildly tangled and your face all hot and ruddy."

Cassie couldn't help laughing. "You make me sound disgusting."

"Maybe to your ears," he said. "But not to mine. I remember thinking what a vibrant, healthy, gutsy woman you were. I wanted you so much that I could scarcely see straight."

Cassie felt a little jolt go through her, but she remained cautious. "I thought you didn't like me at all. And you've spent so much time with Monica..."

"I hardly had much choice there. You insisted that I stay at a distance. You've made quite an issue of that. And of course, Monica has practically followed me everywhere I went."

"I guess I did put you in an awkward spot," she admitted.

"Well, I think we both got ourselves into that trap quite neatly," Jack said. "It was my fault too for teasing you too much at the beginning. Now the question is, can we get ourselves out of the trap? No wait," Jack stopped himself. "Perhaps I'm being presumptuous."

"My response to you is...well, it's hardly neutral, is it Jack? I've never known anything like last night."

"But it's—" Jack broke off as he saw Cassie begin to quake from head to toe. He held her like a baby, cradling her head against his chest. "I'm a damnable man. I've rushed you, Cassie, rushed you far too much. Stop trembling, my sweet. It's going to be all right. I'm going to give you time...*and* distance."

Chapter Ten

BECAUSE DOUG PRESSURED everyone to make up the time they had lost during Monica's illness, Cassie had to work at a frantic pace for the next five days. She was so busy that she hardly talked to anyone. And she worked with such speed and concentration that she had trouble relaxing when the work day was over. As a result, she wolfed down her meals much faster than usual. Then she'd wind up with a stomachache and excuse herself from everyone's company. However, even when she was alone in her room, she couldn't unwind. She'd lie awake half the night, worrying.

At first, she would worry about the day that had just passed. She wondered if she could have done more with certain shots, if perhaps she could have gotten better lighting. Then, of course, her thoughts would always turn to Jack and the fire that he'd started within her. She knew that she couldn't have him. He'd been pleasant, kind—and distant—and she knew no more about how she really felt than she had five days ago. The moments Jack had held her in his power had been so painfully delicious. And she yearned so for his possession, but the nightmare was a warning she had to heed. Where would it all go with him? How would it end?

And, then, the work ended. Cassie could hardly believe that she was free from the grueling routine. There were still some things to be done. She had to do last-minute shots at Hillside and she also needed to develop some prints while she was there. But, the main body of the work was completed.

Back at Hillside, her old room seemed homey and familiar after all the time she had spent in the game park lodges. Deciding to settle in for the few days of their stay, she unpacked all her clothes and put them in the closets and dressers. Then she selected a pair of beige raw silk pants and a hot pink silk shirt, slipped into a pair of matching hot pink sandals, and went to take a look at herself in the mirror. She was delighted to see herself in something besides the jeans and cotton shirts she wore for work. Her reflection made her feel more cheerful and refreshed.

There was a patio near the bar and the main buildings. Cassie decided that it might be fun to go there and sun bathe and relax. In any case, it would be pleasant to sit and do nothing for a change.

She strolled to the patio. Selecting a chaise longue, she sat down and stretched out her legs. She felt very much at peace, watching the birds and the flowers. Closing her eyes, she sighed contentedly.

"Why the satisfied sigh? You haven't even seen what I brought you yet."

It was Jack's voice. Cassie didn't even have to open her eyes to know it. She sat for a moment, remembering the long hours that she'd lain awake thinking about his passionate lovemaking. She realized she was not only in control, but glad to see him. Calmly, Cassie looked up at him with a warm smile of welcome on her lips.

"Now you owe me two," Jack said. "One for getting you away from that rhino. And one for this." Jack held up a bottle of champagne and two glasses.

"Why don't you just let me pay for the champagne and we can even up the score?" suggested Cassie.

"Ah! My dear Ms. Dearborn, I'm hardly going to let you off that easily. Not for the rhino. Besides, I like having you in my debt."

"I've noticed," Cassie said with mock reproach. "But I don't exactly approve of some of your collection methods, Mr. Barton-Hyde."

"I see," Jack said, "I'm in the presence of a true Puritan. Well, let's just say that the champagne is freely given. That is, if you care to do me the honor of joining me?"

"Why not?"

"You really do look quite decorative when you're dressed up," Jack observed, as he ran his eyes over her figure.

Cassie felt a tremor when his eyes were on her. "But I'm not here to decorate the landscape, sir."

"That may not be your purpose, but nonetheless you do it extremely well," he said with an easy smile.

He sat down next to her and poured the champagne. Then he handed her a glass and raised his for a toast.

"What shall it be?" he said.

"To Africa," she replied.

Their glasses clinked and they each took a sip.

"Mmm," said Cassie. "This is just what I needed. Thank you."

Jack didn't say anything right away. He just looked at Cassie thoughtfully. Finally he broke the silence, "Then you really do like it here?"

"Of course," Cassie said.

"I wondered if you did."

Cassie studied him for a moment. Oh, dear, had her toast sounded leading? His next words compounded her troubled embarrassment.

"I can't wait until you see the house," he said.

"What house?"

"*My* house. I live about two miles back into the coffee plantation. I designed it myself with the help of one of the local architects."

"I'll look forward to it," she said, and wondered if he heard the tremor in her voice.

"It's really quite lovely, I think. Doug was up there briefly and he wanted to use the place for some of your shots. I had to tell him that under no circumstances would I permit the whole group to come trooping through the place. I told him that I didn't mind you coming, but that would be it."

"I don't get it," said Cassie suspiciously.

"That's where the darkroom is."

"Oh," Cassie replied. She wasn't sure she wanted to go to Jack's house by herself, but if that was where the darkroom was she didn't have much choice in the matter.

Out of the corner of her eye, Cassie saw Monica walking toward the bar. Then she stopped and looked at Cassie and Jack. For a moment, Cassie thought she saw anger flashing in Monica's eyes. However, if the look was there, it was gone the next moment and covered by a smile.

"Hi, you guys," Monica said, as she hurried over. Then she saw the champagne. "Hey, can I have some?"

"Of course," said Jack, and signaled a waiter to bring another glass for Monica.

The waiter came over and poured some champagne for Monica. Then Cassie turned to Jack with a polite smile.

"You know, Jack," she said. "Now that you have another drinking companion, I think I'd like to take a little walk around the garden. I hope you don't mind."

"I don't suppose it would make much difference if I did," Jack said.

"Oh, come on, Jack," said Monica. "Don't be a spoil-sport. Let Cassie do what she wants."

"Of course I will," he replied.

At that, Cassie got up, taking her drink with her, and meandered into the beautiful garden. Casually, she glanced back at Monica and Jack. She wanted him to know that on this subject, at least, she trusted him.

A few days later, Cassie sat in the den that was just off Jack's darkroom. She had her photographs spread out on the table in front of her and was trying to decide which ones worked the best. Finally, she decided that they'd all turned out well and that Doug ought to be very pleased with the whole set.

This decided, she got up, wandered over to the window, and looked out. There was a beautiful view from the den. She'd stared at it often in the last few days. Just outside, a lawn bordered with oleander bushes stretched down toward a large pond. Beyond the pond were rows and rows of coffee trees.

The view was almost as lovely as the house itself. Cassie hadn't been through the whole place. Jack had offered her a tour, but she'd politely refused and gone straight to the darkroom to work. Yet, as she passed through some of the rooms, she couldn't help noticing how tastefully Jack had furnished his home.

She turned away from the window and started to go back to work. Then she saw that Jack was standing in the doorway, staring at her. Neither of them said anything for a moment. In the silence, Cassie was uncomfortably aware of her desire for him.

Finally, Jack spoke. "I suppose you're getting along fine?"

Cassie just nodded.

"Can I get you anything?" he asked.

Cassie shook her head. "I'll be going in a little while anyway." She nodded toward the pile of prints. "Looks like I've finished up."

"Oh, is this your work?" asked Jack as he crossed over to the pile of pictures.

"Yeah."

"Do you mind if I take a look? I love photography. I'm not much good at it myself, but I've collected some."

"Go right ahead."

He started to go through the prints, looking them over thoughtfully, taking his time with each one. Finally, he turned to Cassie.

"You're really excellent. I had no idea."

"Well, it's nice to know you had such confidence in my abilities," Cassie said lightly. She didn't know whether to be flattered by the compliment or insulted by the fact that he hadn't expected she could do that well.

Suddenly, Jack blushed, which was something Cassie never thought she'd see him do. "That's not what I meant. Of course, I assumed you were talented. I would have been surprised if you weren't, but these are really extraordinary."

Now it was Cassie's turn to blush. "Oh, come on, they're not that great. I'm glad you like them and everything, but..."

"Look at this one," Jack said, holding up a picture of a Kikuyu woman and a little boy. "It's quite wonderful."

"Oh, that," Cassie said. "That's not for the magazine. That's one I took just for myself."

"When did you ever find the time? Did you do this while Monica was sick?"

"No, it was that first morning in Nairobi. I got up early to do some shots of the Nairobi marketplace. Remember when I came running in late..."

"How could I forget? Besides the tart tongue..."

Suddenly, Jack was standing very close to her. Cupping her chin in his hand, he turned her face up to his. His sometimes cold, blue eyes were now shining with warmth. He was watching her in an almost frighteningly intense way.

"You know I want you, don't you?" he whispered hoarsely.

"Jack, I . . ." Cassie trailed off. She'd started to explain some of her misgivings, but then she decided that she didn't need to.

"Answer me," he said urgently. "Do you know how tortured I am with want every time I think of our night together?"

Cassie looked into his eyes boldly. They were filled with desire. "I know. I want you, too, badly."

His strong arms slid around her waist. She didn't resist as he drew her toward him. Then she felt her breasts crushed into the hard muscles of his chest.

"Oh, Cassie! Cassie!" he whispered.

He grasped her firmly against him. Cassie felt as though she were trapped in a vice, he held her so close. Yet, she willingly lost herself in his embrace.

Gently, Jack pressed her down onto the floor. She felt the soft pile of the Oriental rug cushion her back, as he laid her down on it.

"Cassie!" he cried, as he slid his hand over her breast and down her side.

She held him tightly to her. She could hardly believe the joyful rapture of being back in his embrace. As she felt his firm body press against her, she dug her fingers deeply into the muscles of his back. She wanted him to know that her need for him was as intense as his was for her. Hungrily, her lips sought his. She thought of all those lonely nights when she'd lain awake wanting him. And the odd thing was, now that she was in his arms, her need was even sharper than she'd dared to imagine. She reached up and felt the back of his head, ran her hand through his silky dark curls. Every hair seemed to etch a tiny path across her palm.

She was dimly aware of Jack fumbling with the buttons of her shirt. She was about to help him out, then she decided that she'd let him struggle through it. She wanted to savor every moment of their sexuality, all the awkwardness and uncertainty, as well as the strength. But suddenly he was on his feet, pacing away from her while running his fingers distractedly through his hair.

Cassie looked up at him startled, then scrambled to her feet.

"What's wrong? she asked.

"I promised to back off. I . . . I don't break my word, but you do provide a downright temptation! Cassie, have you sorted anything out yet?"

"I . . . not really, Jack."

"Is there anything I can do to make you feel more— I don't know what the word is—more confident with me? Is there anything we can talk about?"

"I don't think discussing things will make a difference at this point."

"I see," said Jack. Hanging his head, he stared down at the pattern on the Oriental rug. Cassie's heart went out to him. She almost ran to comfort him and hold him in her arms.

"I must say," Jack began hesitantly. "I want you to be confident, successful, quite sure you know what you really want."

With that, he walked out of the room. As Cassie watched him go, she felt a sinking feeling in her stomach. The awful feeling of confusion and loneliness came closing back in around her. It was everything she could do to keep from crying out to him to wait. But he was gone.

She started to gather up her prints and go. Hurriedly, she massed all the pictures into a pile. As she did, she kept thinking about how only moments before Jack's hands had held those same pieces of paper.

Suddenly, she sat down at the table and put her head in her hands. She had finally realized that she was in love with him. She knew that love was supposed to make people happy, but for her the very thought of this passion was misery. She'd fought it. She'd struggled with an enormous amount of energy to keep from admitting to herself that she was desperately in love with Jack. She'd tried so hard to keep those passions locked up in her heart in a secret place where even she couldn't see them. Yet, now that she knew she was in love with him, she couldn't avoid the pain that she'd been trying to protect herself from. She began to cry.

She felt an aching longing that could never be released because the situation was so impossible. She knew that she could go to bed with Jack for all her nights in Africa—precious few now. How could she have fallen for a man so far from her home? And how was she ever to erase him from her mind?

Stumbling into the darkroom, she found a tissue and wiped her eyes and blew her nose. She tried to pull herself together, but a fresh wave of sobs shook through her. Grabbing another tissue, she wiped her eyes again. She didn't wanted Jack to see her crying like this. Quickly she gathered the prints and went out the front door. As she hurried away from the house, she glanced back over her shoulder. She thought she saw Jack standing in one of the upstairs windows, but he didn't wave or make any sign that he saw her leaving.

That evening she came into dinner late. She noticed uneasily that Jack was there and snagged into sitting next to Monica. The two of them were deep in conversation, so it was easy for Cassie to avoid their eyes. Hurriedly, she went to sit next to Max and Jill.

"You look nice," said Jill.

"Thanks," Cassie replied. She'd worn a green silk dinner dress that set off her gold hair and gray eyes. She knew she looked especially pretty in it.

She ordered her meal and had just started to eat the first course, when Doug got up. He tapped his spoon against the edge of his glass to get everyone's attention. The group quieted down.

"I have some news for everybody," Doug said. "Thanks to Cassie, Kate and Monica, Barry, Max, Jill, and, of course, last but not least, me, we have some excellent pictures for the magazine."

At this, everybody cheered.

"So," Doug continued. "I just called New York and suggested that we take an extra few days out here to do some shots for the next issue. Unless, somebody has some sort of time problem, another commitment or whatever, we're all going to go down to Malindi on the Kenyan coast. They'll fly the clothes in from New York as soon as I give the go ahead."

Everyone looked around the room expectantly, wondering if there would be some objections. The group seemed to be enthusiastic about the proposal.

Just to make sure, Doug asked, "Is there anybody who can't manage it?"

No one said anything, so that was that. They were going to Malindi.

Cassie sat on the beach, staring out at the Indian Ocean. The two days that she'd been in Malindi had gone surprisingly quickly. She'd thrown herself into her work in an effort to forget about her problems in coming to terms about the situation with Jack. During the day, at least, she'd been able to push him out of her mind. However, times like right now, when the work was over, it was hard to forget him.

She stretched and then found a more comfortable position on the lounge chair. She had on her black string bikini, which was the perfect thing to wear for tanning, though she doubted that she'd get much color since the late afternoon sun wasn't very strong. Taking a sip of her rum punch, she stared out at the ocean. Once again, the image of Jack intruded into her mind and she was filled with painful yearning.

She jumped up and padded down the walkway to her cottage. Beside her the surf pounded steadily against the long sandy beach and the towering palms gently rocked in the breeze. Yet Cassie couldn't bear to look at the beauty of the place. Every time she felt relaxed, her guard would go down and she would think of Jack again. How wonderful it would be to share this with him! It was the perfect place for romance.

After showering, she changed into a black and white cotton dress made of diaphanous cotton scarves. It was one of her favorite dresses because it swirled around her body in a way that was sexy, but never too revealing. It was also the perfect outfit for lounging around in this hot, coastal climate.

She decided that the only sensible thing to do would be to wander down to the lounge to see if any of the others were there. As she had expected, most of the group had stopped in for cocktails. Max and Jill were sitting in one corner; Doug sat at a table with Monica and Kate. Since she would obviously be intruding on Max and Jill, Cassie walked over to Doug's table.

"Hi," she said.

Doug ran an appraising glance over her little black and white dress. "Well, don't you look nice."

"Thank you," said Cassie. She noticed that he seemed to be peering at the diaphanous folds to see if anything was revealed.

"Can I buy you a drink?" he asked.

"Just a ginger ale," Cassie said as she sat down.

"That's all?" Doug asked irritably.

"I had one of those rum punches on the beach today," she replied. "They're awfully strong. I know I couldn't handle another one right now."

He got up and went to the bar to order her drink.

"So how are you guys doing?" Cassie asked the models.

"Kate just got another letter from her fiance," Monica said with a little pout.

"Really?"

"Yes," Kate said demurely. "I really miss him. Can't wait to get home."

"Guess what he said he was going to get her," Monica said enviously.

"What?"

"Diamonds," Monica said. "A carat for every week she's been away."

"Then you'll get your engagement ring and everything!" Cassie said.

"I'm so jealous I could spit," Monica muttered.

Just then Doug came back with Cassie's ginger ale.

"Thank you," she said as she took a sip.

"What were we talking about?" he asked.

"Men," Monica said. Then she added bitterly, "Sometimes I just hate 'em."

"Oh now, Monica," Kate said. "It's foolish to upset yourself like this. Things will work out for you."

"That's easy for you to say," Monica said. "You're getting all those diamonds."

"You'll get diamonds, too," Kate assured her.

"Yeah?" Monica asked. "When?"

"Soon, I'm sure," Kate replied.

"What about us guys?" Doug said. "We don't always get what we want either." He gave Cassie a rather pointed look.

"Boy, this conversation is making me depressed," Monica complained.

"Anything we can do?" Doug asked.

"Yeah," she answered. "You can let me borrow Cassie for a minute."

"Me?" Cassie asked nervously. The last thing she wanted to do right now was to be alone with Monica.

As Monica rose her eyes suddenly widened.

"Oh, my goodness," she said, and popped her hand over her mouth.

Cassie turned to look in the same direction and saw Jack standing in the doorway. Their eyes met. She looked at him searchingly, but she couldn't get a clue as to what he was thinking.

"Jack!" squealed Monica.

She ran to him and threw her arms around him. Everyone else in the group either got up and started over to Jack or waved. Everyone except Cassie. Cassie just stood staring at him.

"What are you doing here?" Monica asked.

"Obviously I came to see everyone," he replied. Then he turned and looked directly at Cassie. "Besides Doug and Cassie still owe me one for saving them from that rhino."

Chapter Eleven

CASSIE GALLOPED ALONG the edge of the Indian Ocean.
She was riding a powerfully built Arabian mare that she
had rented from the local stable, a big feisty bay horse
who loved to run. Cassie had ridden a lot back home in
Ohio so she felt perfectly comfortable.

As the mare thundered down the beach, her hooves
hit the edges of the waves and little sprays of salt water
splattered Cassie's legs and feet. Sometimes the water
splashed as high as her face. But she didn't mind because
it felt so refreshing.

She had chosen to ride bareback, which was the way
that she'd always ridden before, and she could feel the
powerful muscles bunching and releasing under her
knees. Leaning forward, low over the mare's neck, she
threw herself into the frenzy of the run. The horse was
in excellent physical condition, but eventually Cassie
began to notice that the animal was working up a light
sweat. She gently pulled back on one rein, then released.
The mare instantly responded. Cassie signaled again.
The mare slowed to a walk.

Turning around, Cassie started back along the beach
in the direction from which she had come. She had started
out with Doug, Jack, Monica, and Kate, but then she
had decided to gallop ahead on her own. Now she could
see the four of them off in the distance, riding up the
beach toward her.

Loosening the reins, she let the mare stretch out her

neck and walk toward the others at an easy relaxed pace. That way, the horse would have a chance to rest and she would have a chance to think.

Strangely enough, now that Jack was near her, Cassie hadn't been able to approach him. She was paralyzed. She had no ideas for their future—provided he wanted one.

As she got closer to the foursome, she could see Monica perched on her horse gripping nervously at the mane. Kate sat on her horse with the grace of a country-club trained rider. Doug seemed to be intent on showing his horse who was boss. Cassie didn't like that much; she thought he was being needlessly rough on the animal. She glanced at Jack and then quickly looked away again. She thought it ridiculous that just a glance at him could make her skin go hot. Finally she got up the nerve to look at him again. He sat on the horse in an elegant and relaxed manner, but she could tell that he wasn't as skilled a rider as she was. However, he had such thorough knowledge of animals that he seemed to be a natural horseman. He wore a white gauzy shirt, with the collar open and sleeves rolled up. Cassie felt uncomfortable when she looked at his body, because by now she was all too familiar with it's strength and power.

"Cassie!" Doug called out to her.

She waved and urged the mare to trot toward them. There was no way that she could avoid the group's company any more. She decided that she might as well ride up to them and would try to spend most of her time talking to Kate or Monica.

"Cassie, you looked tremendous!" Doug cried, as she approached the group.

Feeling his eyes studying her body, Cassie instantly remembered that the splashing water had soaked her shirt and it clung close to her skin—and she regretted it.

"It's wonderful out here, isn't it?" she said with a big grin.

"Yes, it's a gorgeous day," Kate agreed politely.

"What I find impressive," Jack said with a sexy twinkle in his eye, "is your skill with a horse, Ms. Dearborn. You're really quite magnificent."

"Oh, well..." said Cassie. She hung her head modestly. She felt like a fool for being so shaken up.

Monica smiled at Jack, who was riding next to her. "Let's go back to the lodge and have cocktails or something. I'm getting so sore from this horse, it's pathetic."

"That seems reasonable," Doug said.

"Unless Cassie wants to show off a little more," Monica said bitingly.

Shocked, Cassie looked at Monica. The model was staring at her with a pouty frown. Cassie couldn't believe that Monica would say such an openly hostile thing in front of everybody. "I certainly don't want to delay cocktails," Cassie said sweetly, and they turned and headed back to the lodge.

Jack rode close to her. "May I see you tonight after dinner, Cassie, when no one is apt to be around? I've really come to Malindi to talk to you."

Her throat was dry. Tonight. "Yes, Jack," she murmured. "Of course."

Cocktail hour had lasted far too long for Cassie. She was relieved when the group decided to go into dinner and numbly trailed along. On the outside she was passive, but within she was unaccountably nervous. She ordered another rum punch, hoping it would dull her apprehensiveness.

As she took her first sip, she felt a person leaning toward her and glanced up. Doug seated himself at her side and drew his chair close.

"Enjoying all those rum drinks?"

Cassie realized he was staring at her intently, his body tightly bowed toward her and she felt extremely uneasy. There was something quite different about Doug now.

"I like the drinks fine," she said in reply to his questions.

"You seem to have had quite a few."

"Have I?" said Cassie. "I believe this is only my second."

Doug nodded. "They're awfully strong."

"I guess I do feel a little funny."

"So, we'll all be going back to New York soon," he said trying to make conversation.

"Oh, right," Cassie said. She couldn't think of anything else to say. She wondered if she might be a little drunk.

"We should go out to dinner once we're there," Doug said. "I know a great little Italian place in the East Fifties."

"Italian?" said Cassie faintly. "Oh no, I couldn't." The thought of all that spaghetti made her feel a little queasy.

"Are you all right?" Doug asked.

"Yes," Cassie said. "I think so."

"Food will make you feel better," he said as the waiter brought their dinner.

"Right," said Cassie. She realized that she was definitely feeling tipsy. She wolfed down her food in an effort to counteract the effects of the rum. It helped a little, but she was still feeling a bit disconnected.

It seemed pointless to sit around when she didn't feel very well. She certainly wasn't up to making conversation with anyone nor was she particularly in the mood to sit around chatting. She decided that maybe the easiest thing for her to do would be to go back to her room and relax before she went back to talk with Jack.

Standing up, Cassie nodded to the group. "I think I'm going to turn in for the evening."

She noticed that Jack gave her a startled look.

Ignoring him, Cassie turned and walked out of the dining room. As she headed down the path to her bungalow, she looked out at the ocean. The moon was full and it cast a path of light across the waves. By the time she got to her room, she was so mesmerized by the beauty of the place that she stood outside and looked out at the sea. Leaning up against a palm tree, she pressed her cheek against its smooth bark. Finally she went inside.

Cassie kicked off her shoes, stretched, and looked around the room. Here she was spending another evening alone. During the weeks that she'd been in Africa, she'd begun to get used to her own company. She was at the point where she felt comfortable being on her own.

Just then she heard a knock at the door. Jack! He'd come to her. She'd left the door unlocked, so she called out, "Come on in!"

But it was Doug who opened the door and came into the room. He was carrying a bottle of cold champagne and two glasses. "I thought you might want a little nightcap?"

"No thanks, Doug," Cassie said. "I've already gone over my limit. That's why I turned in early."

"That's crazy," he replied. "I've ordered the champagne. I'm not about to waste it."

Cassie really didn't want to cope with him right now, but it looked like she didn't have much choice. "Doug, I really don't want any champagne. Thanks for thinking of me, but maybe you'd better find someone else to share it."

"I bought it to drink with you," he said with a pout.

"I'm sorry, but I really don't care for any."

Ignoring her remarks, Doug sat down on the edge of the bed and began to uncork the champagne. Cassie could feel her patience running out. She didn't particularly want a showdown with her boss, but if he didn't stop pressuring her, that's exactly what would have to happen.

"Doug," she said, "I meant it. I don't want champagne."

"Sure you do," he said.

"No, I don't."

"Come on, everybody likes champagne."

"I never said I didn't like it. I only told you that I don't really care for any now. I'd like to be left alone."

"But I ordered it!"

"Hey, *I* didn't ask you to bring it," said Cassie irritably. "Seriously, Doug, I've had too much to drink already. I'm very tired and I'd like to go to bed."

"So would I," said Doug. The sexual double entendre was very clear.

"I want to go to bed alone," she said firmly.

"I know that's what you *think* you want, but it isn't what you really want," Doug said insistently.

Cassie could feel the fury starting to well up in her. Since she'd been drinking, her inhibitions were down. "I'll tell you what I really want," she said levelly. "I really want you to get out of here. Right now. I don't want to play any more of these stupid games."

"I'm tired of the games, too, Cassie," he said.

Quickly, he crossed the room and crushed Cassie in a strong embrace. He pressed his mouth against hers so hard that he bruised her lips. Cassie turned her head away from his kiss, but Doug grabbed the back of her neck and forced her lips to meet his.

"Come on, Cassie," he said. "You've been leading me on all this trip."

Gathering all her strength, she pushed him away. "I have *not* been leading you on. I've been doing everything I could to stay out of your way."

"You think you're Miss Tough Lady, don't you? You think you're so great." Doug's face was red with suppressed rage. "But you won't act that way for long, because I know what you like."

"I'd like for you to get out of here. That's what I'd like."

"You pretend. You play a good game. But I know you want me."

"Doug, I don't want you. I've never wanted you. Please, get that into your head."

"You just like to play hard-to-get," Doug said, leering at her.

"Right," said Cassie sarcastically. Then she added, "I've had it with you, Doug. I want you to get out and get out now."

"It seems to me that you already asked me that once before," he replied coolly. "I have no intention of leaving. You may as well get used to that idea."

Suddenly, Cassie felt very threatened. The bungalows were quite a ways apart and she was even farther from the lounge. It was doubtful that anyone would hear her if she screamed. She could try to get out the front door and run away. However, right now Doug was blocking her exit.

Cassie backed down a little, stalling for time. "All right, Doug. Where does that leave us?"

"I'm sleeping with you tonight."

"Doug, forget it."

"I'm going to have what I want. That's all there is to it."

"You sound like a spoiled child," she said contemptuously.

"And you are being unrealistic," he said with a cruel smile.

"What do you mean?" Cassie asked. Her eyes darted urgently toward the door. As if he knew what she was thinking, Doug positioned himself squarely between her and the exit.

"I mean, that we both know what's going on. Now

we can do this nicely and politely." He looked coldly at Cassie. "Or we can put all our cards on the table."

Cassie looked at him defiantly. "I think we stopped being polite long ago."

"Then do you want to know the bottom line?"

"By all means," she said levelly.

"Okay," Doug said. "If you don't sleep with me now, you'll never work for the magazine again."

Cassie felt a cold rage come over her.

Doug went on: "You know I have a lot of influence back in New York. I can make or break your career. If word gets out that you're not cooperative, that you're a troublemaker..."

Finally, Cassie found her voice and interrupted him. "What do you think I am, some kind of prostitute?"

"I'm hoping that you're a sensible woman."

"I'm not selling my sexual services," Cassie said in a loud, angry voice. "I'm a photographer."

"All photographers do a little extra work to keep their business alive."

"Oh really. Even the men?"

"They give me tradeoffs in other ways."

"They find you women?"

"If I ask them to."

"Sounds like a lousy way to run a business, Doug," Cassie said. "I'm surprised that you haven't got more pride than that. Surely, you can find someone who likes you for yourself, not for some little favor you might do them."

With that, she headed straight for the door. When she got to where Doug stood blocking her way, she tried to push him aside. But he grabbed her arms firmly.

"Where do you think you're going?" he asked.

"Since you're not going to leave my room, I am."

"It's not going to be that easy, Cassie," Doug said as he tightened his grip on her arm.

Cassie struggled to pull free. "Let go, Doug. Let go!"

But he held onto her firmly. Cassie remembered from a street safety class that the thumb was the weakest link in a person's grip. She tried to pry Doug's thumbs away from her arms, but he just pushed her hands out of reach of his. She struggled to break loose, but he was a strong, wiry man and she was weak from all those rum drinks.

"Doug, I swear," said Cassie. "I'm going to start yelling like mad if you don't let me go."

"Go on," said Doug. "Go on."

Doug looked at her with a cruel glint in his eyes. He tried to push her toward the bed. There was no doubt in Cassie's mind that he intended to rape her. Her heart started thumping in terror.

She screamed for help over and over again. Her voice was louder than she'd thought. She just prayed that it was loud enough for someone to hear.

Doug pushed her down on the bed. As he did, he let go of her for an instant. Quickly, Cassie scrambled off the bed and bolted for the door.

She'd almost made it outside when he grabbed the skirt of her dress. Cassie felt it give and tear loose from the top. She hoped that it would tear completely free, so that she could get away. However, it held.

With a savage yank, Doug pulled her back toward him. Cassie reached up to poke him in the eyes, but he shoved her onto the bed before she could do any damage.

Again, she screamed for help as loud as she could. Desperately, she looked around the room for something to fight with. Seeing a lamp on the bedside table, she picked it up and held it ready.

"You want to get rough, eh?" Doug hissed viciously.

Cassie sensed that he might really try to hurt her. Still, she held her ground.

Just then, somebody kicked the bungalow door open. Cassie saw Jack's tall muscular frame in the entrance.

Immediately, Doug dropped his menacing attitude and tried to look casual. His pose wasn't at all convincing. Cassie was still crouching on the bed with the lamp poised, ready to strike.

Jack looked from Doug to Cassie, then back to Doug. The glint in his eye indicated he was ready to murder. "I suppose our friend Ms. Dearborn has some particular reason for wanting to hit you with a lamp?"

Doug just looked down at the ground and shrugged. "Well?"

Doug didn't say anything. He just started for the door. Grabbing his arm, Jack pulled him roughly to a standstill.

"I'd like to know what you were up to, Mr. Tyler."

"It's between me and Cassie."

"Not any more it's not," Jack said.

Even though he spoke with a calm, clipped precision, Cassie could see that he was violently angry. The veins on his neck and arms were distended as though they were bursting with rage. His cold, blue eyes glared at Doug venomously.

"We were just having a little fun," said Doug contritely.

"Oh, really?" Jack said, his voice rising in anger. "Ms. Dearborn? Were you having fun?"

Quickly, Cassie shook her head. She realized that she was frozen in the same spot, clutching the lamp, and she didn't really feel like setting it down as long as Doug was in the room.

Abruptly, Jack grabbed Doug by the shirt and flung him against the wall of the room. He hit the wall harder than Cassie would have expected. She realized that there must be tremendous power in Jack's sure and supple movements.

"That hurt," Doug whimpered.

"Good," Jack said through a clenched jaw. "That's exactly what I intended."

"I could press charges."

"Go right ahead. I'm sure Ms. Dearborn will be happy to testify."

Doug gave Cassie an uneasy look. She glared back at him. She wanted him to know that she felt no mercy for him.

Jack seized Doug's collar again and held him pinned to the wall. "In the meantime," he said, "if I ever catch you near Cassie again—or forcing your loathsome presence on any woman, for that matter—I'll be happy to show you how much damage I can really do."

Doug just stared nervously at Jack.

"Is that perfectly clear?" Jack asked.

Doug didn't say anything.

"I said any questions?"

Doug shook his head. With that, Jack hurled him out of Cassie's room. She heard a thrashing sound as he crashed against some bushes.

Then Jack turned to her. Cassie still crouched, holding the lamp. "I suppose you intend to carry that lamp around with you all night?"

Cassie looked at the lamp, then smiled and set it down.

"Are you all right?" he asked.

"Yes," she said, finding her voice at last.

"You're sure?"

She nodded.

"Your dress is all torn up," said Jack. "It's too bad. I liked you in that quite a bit. I'll see if I can't get Doug to pay for it. If not, I'll buy you a new one."

"Please don't," said Cassie quickly. "I'd just as soon throw the dress out and forget this ever happened."

Cassie looked up at him and saw that tender expression that she had come to love. She felt her stomach lurch because of poignant response to his gentleness.

"Hold me?" she asked.

Reaching out, Jack put his arm around her. She lay

her head on his shoulder. She knew a peaceful feeling of security, and then she fell asleep in his arms.

Coming full awake with a start, Cassie realized she was being watched.

Jack looked at her with an ironic twinkle in his eye. "Now don't tell me you're sorry I'm here—or that I showed up. I could have sworn you were glad to see me last night."

She smiled. "You seem to be my cavalry. Always arriving just in the nick of time. How did you know to come when you did?"

"We were supposed to have a little chat after supper, remember? You left dinner in such a rush that I wondered what was going on. I wanted to see you, so . . ."

Jack trailed off. He stared at Cassie. Unable to return his gaze, she looked away quickly.

"I'm going to get dressed," she said hurriedly. Before Jack could protest, she grabbed a pair of jeans and a hand embroidered peasant shirt out of her suitcase. She went into the bathroom and changed. Once again, Cassie was grateful for her easy-to-care-for hair. She ran a brush through it a couple of times. Then she brushed her teeth, washed her face, and put on a little makeup. When she came out again, she noticed that Jack was watching her anxiously.

"Stay here," he said.

"Ordering me around again?"

"I'm sorry," he said. "Please wait for me. I want to wash up, but I don't want you to go running off in the meantime."

"I'll wait," she promised.

Jack went into the bathroom. He came out only moments later. It was as though he didn't quite trust her out of his sight. Cassie found his vulnerability charming. She almost threw caution to the winds to tell him he could have whatever he wanted from her. However, she knew she had to hold herself back, because she could be feeling completely unsure of him again within minutes.

"I'd like to have that talk now," he said.

Cassie felt a nervous jolt go through her. She had a feeling that unless she managed to have this conversation at a reasonable distance from her bed, she wouldn't be able to concentrate at all.

"Okay," she said. She thought her voice sounded jittery. "Okay, we can talk. But first, I just have to have my morning coffee. Can't have a serious conversation without it. We can just run up to the lounge. Have a little breakfast. There's good coffee here. Maybe not as good as what you grow on your plantation. I don't know..."

Again, Cassie caught herself jabbering nervously. She stopped and stared at the ground.

"All right," Jack said. "We'll go to the lounge. I'm willing to do anything, as long as you'll be willing to listen to me."

With that, he went to the door of the bungalow and opened it. It was still early and the sun was low over the ocean, the breeze soft and light—the makings of an absolutely perfect day.

"Well, if it isn't the last of the all-time floozies! And here you've been pretending to be my friend!"

Turning around, Cassie and Jack saw Monica. She was glaring venomously at Cassie.

"Boy, oh boy, Cassie," Monica said angrily. "I really didn't think you were the type, you know. I thought you were a pretty decent person. I never would have told you my secrets and stuff, if I'd known you were after him, too."

"I think you have it all wrong, Monica," Cassie said.

"I have it wrong. Oh sure. You come out of your room with Jack bright and early in the morning and you don't expect me to believe that you were after the guy?" said Monica. Her skin was turning pink with anger.

"I wasn't after him," Cassie said. "It was just one of those things that happen."

"Right! You just accidentally on purpose snaked my boyfriend."

"I didn't snake him. It wasn't like that at all."

"Oh no?" Monica asked. "Then what were you doing spending the night together?"

"Nothing."

"You're a floozie, Cassie. A two-bit, cheap-tailed floozie," Monica accused. "Boy, if I'd known what kind of person you are I would have been a hell of a lot more careful. I just hope a lot of terrible stuff happens to you so that you're good and sorry for what you did."

"Monica," said Cassie, her temper rising. "Why don't you just settle down."

"Oh, shut up, Cassie!" Monica shrieked. Then she turned to Jack. "Boy, you sure are some kind of swine, Jack."

"Really?"

"You led me on!" Monica said insistently.

"My dear young woman, I'm truly sorry that I wasn't able to fit into your plans for me," he said levelly. "You see, I make my own plans for my life."

"Clever, Jack," Monica said. "You think you're real hotsy-totsy, don't you?"

"I wish I were," Jack said. "But I have to admit I'm just a fumbling mortal like everyone else."

"Not me," Monica insisted. "I'm not such a fumbling mortal as all that. I'll bet you guys had a real good laugh at me last night. I'll bet you just stayed awake chuckling about how you put one over on old Monica. Well, I've got news for you. I'm going to get even. I'm sure going to get even."

With that, she wheeled and sped toward the lounge. Cassie turned to Jack.

"Go after her. Explain what really happened."

"But I don't owe her any explanation," he said.

"Jack, her feelings are hurt."

"I realize that and I'm sorry. However, I can't really be responsible for Monica's reactions."

Cassie felt herself flaring with anger . . . and fear. This was exactly the response she feared from Jack, that she would commit herself to him wholeheartedly and then he would withdraw from the situation when it pleased him.

"Jack, that is so cruel," she cried. "How can you be so callous to her. Obviously she cares for you."

"That's highly debatable," said Jack, raising his eyebrows quizzically. "But please, let's stop worrying about Monica now and get down to our chat."

"This *is* our so-called chat! And I don't want to forget about Monica. I think you treated her unfairly."

"I don't want to talk about Monica," Jack insisted. "I want to talk about you."

"How can I stop thinking about Monica? Poor thing's probably up in the lounge crying her eyes out this very minute."

"Good point. I don't think we'll ever get to have a serious talk as long as Doug and Monica and the rest of them are around to distract us. Let's go off somewhere alone."

"Absolutely not," Cassie said. "We'll have this out right here."

"But, it's not going to work here," Jack insisted. "We'll go down to Mombasa. I know just the place."

"No way," she said.

"I'm afraid it's the only way."

He lifted her up across his shoulders fireman style

before she had time to protest.

"Very funny. Put me down," she said.

"That's out of the question, my dear."

"I mean it, Jack."

"So do I," he said as he started walking with her, carrying her out toward the parking lot.

"I'll kick and scratch if you don't put me down," she said.

"And I'll tickle you until you're bright scarlet if I feel so much as one fingernail."

"I'll scream."

"Ah! I see. And who's going to rescue you? Doug?"

Cassie immediately saw the humor in the whole thing and chuckled softly. "Maybe Barry?" she suggested in a small voice.

"I wouldn't bank on that, my dear."

Looking around, Cassie saw that they were nearing the parking lot. She also noticed that Doug, Monica, and some other people were just coming out of the lounge.

The sight of a man carrying a woman fireman's style through the parking lot was rare at that particular resort, and people immediately commented on them. Cassie heard Monica yell something, but before the hubbub could increase, Jack tossed her onto the front seat of the jeep. Then he jumped in beside her and they drove away.

Cassie realized suddenly how incredibly relieved she was to be away from the pressures of Monica and Doug and the rest of the group and decided Jack was wise to get both of them out of there like this.

"Where are we going?" she asked.

"Mombasa."

"What's there?"

"A friend's apartment," he said. "Let's wait until we get there to talk. I don't want driving to distract me from the conversation. What I want to talk about is too important."

They drove south along the coast. Cassie was happy

to just lean back against the seat and feel the wind blowing through her hair. She was glad they weren't talking. It gave her a chance to savor Jack's company without any feeling of pressure.

Finally they reached the coastal city of Mombasa. Cassie could feel her heart beating faster as she realized that confrontation was so near. She was so preoccupied with what might happen between her and Jack that she barely got a sense of the city itself.

She was vaguely aware of throngs of people with different styles of dress. There were Arabs wearing beaded hats and vests. Hindus wore either Western clothes or traditional Indian clothes. The Moslem women were covered with flowing black garments, which was a style of dress that Cassie found rather sad and dull. Her favorites were the kangas worn by African women, bright little dresses wrapped around the body just below the armpit and falling to the mid-calf.

Carefully, Jack maneuvered the jeep through the narrow streets of the old city. They passed Indian women selling beautiful gauzy, gold-embroidered saris. Arab merchants drank coffee out of copper pots and argued about the prices of brass-fitted chests. Goldsmiths and tinsmiths boasted about the value of their wares to customers.

Finally, Jack pulled up beside a tall, quaint building that had ornamental balconies which looked out over the street. He parked the jeep and got out.

"My friend has a suite of rooms in here," he said.

"He just lets you use them?" Cassie asked as she jumped down from the jeep.

"She," Jack corrected.

Cassie looked at him with alarm.

"Don't worry, my dear, Lilliana was a friend of my mother's. She practically helped raise me. It's hardly a romantic interest."

"So she just lets you bring women into her apartment."

"It's not quite as coarse as you make it sound. Lil-liana's a writer. She's lecturing in Europe. I told her I'd look in on the place." Then Jack looked at her levelly. "You seem to think of me as some sort of rake, Ms. Dearborn."

"For heaven's sake, Jack."

"I suppose there are a number of men who would find that image flattering," he said. "However, I don't happen to be one of them. That's one of the things I wanted to talk to you about."

"Okay," said Cassie. She could feel her throat getting dry with nervousness.

"Shall we go in?" he asked.

She nodded and then followed him up a narrow stair-way to Lilliana's apartment. Jack opened the door and they went in. Cassie was shocked by the sumptuousness of the place. It was all decorated in the Arabic style, with lots of cushions and rich brocade wall hangings. Thick Oriental rugs cushioned the floor. Brass Arabic tables and lamps added a rich sheen of reflected light. Persian miniatures and valuable Oriental porcelains were tastefully and discreetly arranged around the room.

"Your friend has marvelous taste," Cassie said.

"Yes," Jack agreed. "It's very different from what I've done with Hillside. However, I think my style would range in the same vein as Lilliana's if I lived in Mom-basa."

"Yes, I think mine would, too."

Raising his eyebrows, Jack gave her an amused smile. "Now," he said with a wave of his hand, "supposing you sit down on that divan and tell me why you've been running away from me—and yourself—all this time."

Cassie felt cornered. A moment of truth was at hand. She sat down on the low, Arabic divan and cupped her chin in her hands. She didn't know where to begin.

"Please, Cassandra," Jack said in a low pleading

voice. "I think I have some idea what the problem is, but you must help me. I'm not a mind reader, much as I'd like to be."

"Jack," she said, taking a deep breath and steeling herself to be courageous, "you're beginning to . . . to mean far too much to me. I want to see you every minute of the day. I want to talk to you, even hear your wise-cracks . . . and, you must know, to make love with you."

"Darling," he cried and rushed to embrace her. "You know I feel the same."

"Please, please move away," she begged. "I . . . I can't even get words out straight—much less thoughts—when you're so near."

"A request with which I'll comply for only a very limited time, Cassie." Jack's face was glowing with happiness.

"But, dear Jack," she said softly, "I'm afraid of all this . . . afraid of you and of me. It's so sudden; you're still a relative stranger to me and I . . ." She broke off and chewed her lower lip. Jack waited patiently until she composed her thoughts. "I'm trying to build my life, make something of myself professionally, rediscover my values."

"We've talked about what you've been through, Cassie. And trust me that I know what you're feeling, thinking. But, my sweet, there is some chemistry between us that has nothing to do with sorting through one's life to come to conclusions. I've realized that over the last days. Realized it painfully. I think both of us knew—I sooner than you, of course—that it was nothing short of a miracle to have come together. There is an undeniable bond between us, a bond I know is called attraction and more—love."

Tears welled in Cassie's eyes. She was unable to stop them and they spilled slowly down her cheeks. "Yes, yes," she whispered. "I do love you."

Jack came to her then and held her tenderly. "Whoever said that getting one's life in order had to be done alone? Won't you let me help, Cassie? And won't you help me in return? We need each other, darling."

She could only sob, then. A dam had burst inside her and she felt safe, at home at last in Jack's arms. However long it lasted, her relationship with Jack would be richly rewarding, deeply comforting and excitingly adventuress. Did she dare demand more than what he offered? Did she dare demand lifelong commitment? No, she told herself sternly. Who could see beyond tomorrow? Who could make lifelong promises and be sure they could be fulfilled?

He kissed her then with such fierce reassurance that her heart leapt in her breast.

"Oh, I want you," she cried as she ran her fingers along the sinewy muscles of his back.

"And you're going to have me," he murmured, punctuating each word with a tiny kiss along her neck. "As often as you want."

Sliding down onto the divan, they pressed their bodies close together. Jack slipped his hand under Cassie's peasant blouse. His fingers eagerly sought her breast. The other hand struggled to release the buttons of her skirt. Then he gently eased his mouth down from her neck and across her shoulders to caress her breasts.

With a soft little cry of pleasure, Cassie closed her eyes and gave in to the deliciousness of the sensation. She slid her hands across Jack's shoulders, savoring the feel of every bulging muscle.

Suddenly, a wave of impatience arose within her. She felt an impetuous need to feel Jack's flesh against hers. Eagerly, she reached down and undid the buttons of his shirt, then pulled it off and let her fingers glide along the smooth muscles of his chest.

Then she began to kiss his shoulders. She wanted to explore every part of him. He moaned softly and doubled his caresses when he felt her eager responses. But suddenly he pulled back, grinning at her. "Let's go back to Malindi and pack your things," he said. "It seems only right."

"Right?" she echoed, a bit stunned at the loss of his touch.

"We'll have come full circle then. After all, my first real contact with you was when I had to stuff your lingerie into your suitcase."

The twinkle in Jack's eye made Cassie feel she might die for love of him.

"Actually, dear Cassie, I think you could have quite a viable career in Africa." His voice quavered.

A smile threatened to erupt and she sternly repressed it. Poor Jack, so sure of himself usually, squirming now and anxious. She went weak and had to put this lovable man out of his misery. "Jack, are you asking me to stay in Africa?"

"It . . . it would be a good place for you to work. You wouldn't have to deal with people like Doug and you do have the most marvelous feel for the people and the countryside."

"I didn't ask for a report on job prospects, darling. My question was do *you* want me to stay."

Putting his hands on her cheeks, then cupping her face gently, he said fervently, "Yes. Forever. With me."

Cassie twined her arms around his body. She had it all, even the commitment she hadn't dared hope for. "Oh, my darling, it's what I want more than anything."

As Jack scooped her up in his arms, rose and carried her to the bedroom, Cassie nuzzled close against his powerful shoulder. She was certain at last. Something deep inside told her that all the pain and problems of the past had been preparation . . . for Jack, the person she'd been searching for all along. She thanked God for this gentle friend, this rugged lover she'd dreamed of finding all her life.

Second Chance at Love

QUESTIONNAIRE

1. How many romances do you *read* each month? _____

2. How many of these do you *buy* each month? _____

3. Do you read primarily
   - ☐ novels in romance lines like SECOND CHANCE AT LOVE
   - ☐ historical romances
   - ☐ bestselling contemporary romances
   - ☐ other _____

4. Were the love scenes in this novel (this is book # _____)
   - ☐ too explicit
   - ☐ not explicit enough
   - ☐ tastefully handled

5. On what basis do you make your decision to buy a romance?
   - ☐ friend's recommendation
   - ☐ bookseller's recommendation
   - ☐ art on the front cover
   - ☐ description of the plot on the back cover
   - ☐ author
   - ☐ other _____

6. Where did you buy this book?
   - ☐ chain store (drug, department, etc.)
   - ☐ bookstore
   - ☐ supermarket
   - ☐ other _____

7. Mind telling your age?
   - ☐ under 18
   - ☐ 18 to 30
   - ☐ 31 to 45
   - ☐ over 45

8. How many SECOND CHANCE AT LOVE novels have you read?
   - ☐ this is the first
   - ☐ some (give number, please _____)

9. How do you rate SECOND CHANCE AT LOVE vs. competing lines?
   - ☐ poor
   - ☐ fair
   - ☐ good
   - ☐ excellent

10. Check here if you would like to
    - ☐ receive the SECOND CHANCE AT LOVE Newsletter

. . . .

Fill-in your name and address below:

name:_____

street address:_____

city_____ state_____ zip_____

Please share your other ideas about romances with us on an additional sheet and attach it securely to this questionnaire.

PLEASE RETURN THIS QUESTIONNAIRE TO:
SECOND CHANCE AT LOVE, THE BERKLEY/JOVE PUBLISHING GROUP
200 Madison Avenue, New York, New York 10016